The Stones are

*'You are the one,' he said. 'You mus. _
waking. You must save us.'*

Phelim was the only one, they said, the only one who could save the world from the Hatchlings of the Stoor Worm. The Stoor Worm, who had been asleep for aeons, was beginning to waken. The dreadful sounds of war had roused it, and now its Hatchlings were abroad, terrorizing the people who had forgotten all about them, forgotten all the ancient magics.

But how could Phelim, who was only a boy, after all, save the world from all these dreadful monsters? And where could he find the Maiden, the Fool, and the Horse who were supposed to help him? As Phelim leaves his home and sets out on his quest, the words ring in his ears: 'You are the one. To stop the Worm waking. To do what must be done.'

GERALDINE MCCAUGHREAN took a degree in education at Christ Church College, Canterbury. She worked for some years for a London publisher on a variety of projects, including children's partworks, and now writes full time. Among her other books for Oxford University Press are *A Little Lower than the Angels*, *A Pack of Lies*, *Gold Dust*, *Plundering Paradise*, and *Forever X*.

The Stones are Hatching

Other books by Geraldine McCaughrean

One Thousand and One Arabian Nights
Saint George and the Dragon
The Canterbury Tales
El Cid
The Odyssey
Moby Dick
A Little Lower than the Angels
A Pack of Lies
Gold Dust
Plundering Paradise
Forever X

The Stones are Hatching

Geraldine McCaughrean

OXFORD
UNIVERSITY PRESS

OXFORD
UNIVERSITY PRESS

Great Clarendon Street, Oxford OX2 6DP

Oxford University Press is a department of the University of Oxford.
It furthers the University's objective of excellence in research, scholarship,
and education by publishing worldwide in

Oxford New York

Athens Auckland Bangkok Bogotá Beunos Aires Calcutta
Cape Town Chennai Dar es Salaam Delhi Florence
Hong Kong Istanbul Karachi Kuala Lumpur Madrid Melbourne
Mexico City Mumbai Nairobi Paris São Paulo Singapore
Taipei Tokyo Toronto Warsaw

with associated companies in *Berlin Ibadan*

Oxford is a registered trade mark of Oxford University Press
in the UK and in certain other countries

British Library Cataloguing in Publication Data available

ISBN 0 19 271797 9

Cover illustration by David Wyatt

Printed and bound in Great Britain by
Biddles Ltd, www.Biddles.co.uk

For Michèle and Tim

All the creatures, dangers, legends, and magics
described in this book were,
until very recently,
accepted as real and true by ordinary people
living and working in a civilized and Christian Europe.

1

Something Coming

Phelim had always thought there must be more to magic than rabbits or handkerchiefs—that if it existed at all, it would be too large to palm or to hide up your sleeve. If it existed, it would be something too serious for just a laugh and a clap, too scary to carry about in a trunk. Sometimes, when the winter air turned to a puff of smoke in his mouth, or hail reclinkered the garden path, he suspected there was magic at work. But there was no proving or disproving it. His sister Prudence said there was a rational explanation for everything: no room for magic in her world. Phelim was not so sure. Ghosts might have something to do with it, he thought. Phelim believed in ghosts—at least, he believed in ghostly cats.

Prudence had said 'no cats'. He had asked her time and time again, but she went on saying 'no cats'. She was categorical. So Phelim had *imagined* himself a cat—a smart tortoiseshell one which purred and rubbed against his legs. He had even gone so far as to put down a saucer of real milk beside the stove one night, after Prudence had gone to bed. And in the morning the saucer had been drunk dry.

Every evening since then Phelim had set down a saucer of milk beside the range. Long after his imaginary cat had strayed out of mind, the saucer continued to be licked dry, though there was never a window of the house left open, never a strand of fur on the settee, never a pawprint on the flagstone floor.

At first the notion of a ghost cat had scared Phelim, but time had dulled the fright and he had found himself feeding the ghost cat as part of his bedtime routine: scrub the table, wipe the paint-pots, clean the brushes, set the breakfast table, rake out the stove, feed the ghost cat, clean his teeth, make up his bed. He had never actually seen the ghost cat, but then he had never actually seen dirt on his teeth and still he went on cleaning them.

But when he saw the stove, he knew at once that something worse than ghosts had happened in the night. He came downstairs and found the stove pushed out from the wall— the whole massive cast-iron, five-door range—and all the rest of the furniture piled up against the front door. The table had been up-ended to cover the window, so that the room was very dark, and all of Prudence's lead soldiers were scattered on the rush mat. His foot had crumpled one before he had time to realize. Phelim gathered up the rest, gently clasping them to his chest for want of a flat surface.

'One more,' said a small man who emerged, clarted with grease, from behind the range. The creature handed him a soldier. Phelim naturally assumed that he must be dreaming.

'I hate dreams like that,' he said. 'You think you've woken up and got out of bed and dressed—and then you have to do it all over again, because you only dreamt it.'

But when Phelim shut his eyes and opened them again, the scene did not go away. In fact now that his eyes were adjusting to the gloom, he could see other figures in the room, stark-naked men and women about as tall as his waist, shaggy and matted with filth. Their eyes looked out at him, full of terror, from under low, sloping foreheads.

'What *are* these?' asked the creature, nodding at the lead soldiers in Phelim's hands. 'Talismans? Do they guard the house?'

Phelim looked around. He could see a dozen hot cross buns had been threaded on to wire and hooked to the roof beam.

2

Hot cross buns? It was August not Easter. There was a strong smell of herbs and spices, too, and bits of the garden had been brought indoors—not vases of flowers or decorative grasses, but whole clumps of torn up shrubbery, the roots dripping black earth as they lay across the kitchen chairs. Phelim had not brought them in, and his sister was not at home.

He suddenly realized that the people in the room were staring at him, waiting for him to speak. The question about the lead soldiers had required an answer.

'Talismans? No. Just toys,' he said, showing two fistfuls of figures. 'My sister paints them. For a living. That's how we live.' The people sitting on the flagstones all breathed out sighs and slumped a little closer to the floor. There had to be a rational explanation for all this, all these, thought Phelim. His sister would have known what it was.

'What are you *doing* here?' Phelim pleaded. He meant everyone, all of them, but only the creature replied.

'I have to come out. Domovoy cannot hide behind his stove in time like this. Stove is not saving me.' His skin was stained grease-brown by the tarry black stickiness which builds up around cookers. He too was naked. 'And must try . . . ' he gave a helpless shrug . . . 'Must try to save the house.'

'Save it? From them?' Phelim cocked his head towards the cavemen and women.

'No, no! Your glashans? What harm glashans? They mind your fields like I mind your house. How can I turn them away? With what is coming? No, no! I try to save house from the Others. The Hatchlings. But I cannot. Too many. You must. Only you can save us now, Jack o' Green!'

Phelim felt stupid and slow. He felt as if his brains had been sewn up in a bag and thrown over a wall. He had been transported, in his sleep, to some country whose language he did not speak and where everybody had shrunk. He made a last desperate effort to wake up.

'Jacko? I'm not Jacko. That explains it! You have the wrong person . . . I'd like you all to go now, please. You shouldn't be here. My sister wouldn't like it.' And he began pulling apart the barricade, setting chairs back on their feet. 'I'm sorry. I'm not the person you're looking for. You've come to the wrong house. Sorry.'

Just at that moment something threw itself against the door, something big and frenzied and throttling on rage.

The latch rattled and the pile of furniture swayed, and the animal outside continued to bark with insane hysteria at being kept from its meat.

'Black Dog!' cried a glashan.

'Barguest!'

'Tchi-co!'

'Moddey Dhoo!'

'Black Shuck!'

'Padfoot!'

The people on the floor tried to cram themselves into the cupboard of the dresser, into the larder, behind the door. Phelim noticed that six or seven could pack themselves between the potato bin and the wash basket; they must be far smaller than he was himself.

Outside he pictured an Alsatian broken loose from its kennel, maltreated perhaps and starving. He thought of the police, but they were ten miles away in Somerton. The dog's breath rasped in its throat like a hacksaw; its claws scrabbled paint off the door in crackling sheets. When it barked, the glass of the wall-lights shook. Five, six, seven times it hurled itself against the door and then, when the bolts held, fell back and prowled around the house slavering over the spilled dustbin, setting small plant pots rolling, clawing at the brittle roofing-felt covering the cellar door. Phelim felt his own shanks shaking, his feet and palms melting like butter. He was glad these people—whoever they were— had come inside in time. 'This is a nightmare,' he said aloud.

4

'Everyone dreams Black Dog,' said the domovoy, turning through every point of the compass as his large ears followed the noise around the cottage walls. The hound had climbed on to the sloping roof of the coalbunker now.

Phelim knew he had to move. He knew he had to do more than wait for the dog to scratch or climb its way into the house and come ravening down the stairs. He rushed up the staircase on hands and feet, sobbing with the exertion, and threw open both bedroom doors to check that the windows were shut tight. He went over and pressed his face against the dirty glass, trying to catch a squinnying glimpse of the dog below—the hound besieging his sister's cottage. Good job she was away; Prudence was not fond of animals at the best of times.

But Phelim could not see; the dog was too close in against the house, clawing at the brickwork. All he could see was the overturned chicken house crushed into splintery shards, the chickens lying about like torn-off scarlet dahlia heads. Sunrise had drawn up a dense white mist off the wet valley, but he could just make out a couple of figures picking their way across the bald paddock and the meadow overrun with heather. Where were they coming from? Here, in the most dismally lonely corner of nowhere, suddenly there were strangers—and just at the worst possible time. He must warn them. He must shout a warning! Phelim dislodged the window catch and thumped the heel of his hand against the frame. Flakes of old paint showered down on to his wrist and the sill. Cobwebs thick as chewing gum stretched and broke as he pushed the window wide.

'Dog! Dog! Mad dog! Get away!' he bawled.

None of the figures moving across the landscape so much as looked towards the house. And now he looked more carefully, he saw that they were not heading for the house, but ambling by, moving east. One looked as tall as a tree, the other might not be human at all, but some kind of animal. He leaned a little forward through the open window for a better look.

The black muzzle came up towards him, like a breaching whale surfacing under a whaler. Warmly stinking breath engulfed his head as the Black Dog leapt upward into his face. Its muzzle was closed for the leap, but a yellow grappling hook of front incisors pushed forward through the lips and snagged in the wool of his jersey. He did not feel the bite. His brain was taken up with the eyes, the yellow eyeballs foaming phosphorescence, searing themselves into his memory, leaving twin scars.

Then the dog was falling away from him, dangling from his sleeve, teeth tangled in unravelling wool. It was vast—big as a heifer or a lion. Phelim's feet were jerked off the floor, and he felt the pegs of the window-fastening driving into his stomach as he was pulled out of the window. He just managed to grab the sill, but it was rotten—crumbly as dry bread. He spread his legs to wedge himself in the opening and, as the dog landed on its haunches, the strain on his sleeve relented. But he was bound now to the beast, connected to it by an artery of navy wool as complex as the veins in an eye.

It rose towards him again without recoiling for the spring, its hind legs unflexing, its ears cracking as it twisted its head from side to side to be free of the wool. It all seemed to happen so slowly: Phelim had time to take in the broken milk bottle on the lawn, the holes in the garden bed where the bushes had been wrenched up, the marigolds raining down in a shower of maroon and yellow velvet from the next window along, and he had time to think, Marigolds?

The domovoy was rending the flowers out of the window-box and pelting the dog with both marigolds and fistfuls of dry earth.

The Black Dog faltered in its leap, its body snaking in spasms, as if electrocuted, and dropped down again on to all

6

fours. Its snarl was massive—a rip-saw growl embracing the whole valley in its hatred. The domovoy was throwing anything that came to hand now—hairbrushes, picture frames, shoes, and vases. Phelim made his shoulders small and let the pullover slide over his head; it flopped down on to the dog's back. Then Phelim dragged himself back through the window into the bedroom and ploughed his head under the darkness of his quilt so as to shut out the sights and sounds.

Later—he had no idea how much later—the quilt was lifted and the domovoy stood looking at him impassively. 'That is Black Dog,' he said. 'Marigolds are good magic, but marigolds are gone now. Now there is only you.'

'You are good boy. You feed me. Milk is better than nothing. Most do not feed their domovoy ever.'

After Black Dog, the domovoy was hardly frightening at all. For all his filth, he had the perfect white teeth and strong nails of someone who drinks plenty of milk. His stomach growled continually, though, from hunger. 'Please! Help yourself!' Phelim urged, waving his hands towards the cupboards.

'I do,' said the domovoy. 'Also I feed your glashans.' And he heaved the hessian sack of potatoes out of the larder and began distributing them raw to the men and women huddled by the cold stove. At once the glashans began to gnaw on the potatoes ravenously, spitting peel and mud in at the open doors of the stove. 'Rightly, you should feed them yourself. They tend your fields. And glashans make good friends, bad enemies.'

Shaken as he was by the dog attack, Phelim was careful how he answered. He had the wit, for instance, not to say, 'I never fed you. I never knew you existed.' He sensed the offence he would give if he said that the saucer of milk put down nightly had really been meant for a ghost cat. Thanks to

7

the milk, the creature had withheld his malice and the malice of the glashans outside, too. The only trouble was that the creature-from-behind-the-stove seemed now to be expecting something more from Phelim.

'I'm afraid there's been a mistake . . . ' Phelim began nervously. 'Just now. You called me Jacko. My name's not Jacko. My *father* was—well, he was John, really, but Jack sometimes, well, usually really, but I don't much remember, me. I'm—'

'Father. Son. What difference?' said the domovoy who seemed troubled by the length and pointlessness of Phelim's sentences.

'Well, to start with, I'm eleven years old . . . ' he began, but the domovoy cut him short.

'To start with? Younger, surely? A baby, to start with. Grandfather and grandson fill up the same space. Why do you question it? You are the one.'

The glashans murmured in agreement, not because they understood the words: they were simply picking up on the tone of the domovoy's voice. Their eyes glimmered expectantly, rheumy with infection but alert as wild animals.

'The one? What one? Which one? I'm not—'

'To make the journey,' snapped the domovoy impatiently. 'To stop the Worm waking. To do what must be done.'

The kitchen door had been unearthed from its barricade, and now the domovoy was busily stuffing things into a pillowcase from the ironing basket. He seemed to be acquainted with every corner of the kitchen: where to lay hands on what he wanted. But then he had clearly been helping himself to things for years. Was he packing now, on Phelim's behalf?

'I'm sorry,' said Phelim, 'but I can't go anywhere. My sister left me here to look after the house. She paints, you know. These. I told you.' He picked up one of the lead figures. His sister Prudence was away delivering her monthly quota of painted lead soldiers to a toy company in Oakington. Phelim helped her with her work (though she said he was more hindrance than help).

The glashans shuffled across the floor and, before he could stop them, their hands darted out and picked up a dozen of the figurines. Like babies they needed to hold a thing to make sense of it—hold it to their mouths, bite into its substance. They were making bite marks in the soft metal. Prudence would be livid.

The domovoy held out the pillowcase to Phelim who was sufficiently intrigued to look inside. He could see a horse brass, some twigs, the last remaining marigold, a hot cross bun, the remains of the Sunday joint, and a few coins and misshapen pebbles. He looked, then put the pillowcase down on the floor. The domovoy looked irritated.

'A cat's sneeze to blow you on your way! Time is wasting. Every moment the stones are hatching, the Worm is waking!'

They were crowding round him now, jostling and pressing up against him like a flock of sheep. A sweet, outdoor stench rose off them, of rotting vegetation and manure, except for the domovoy who smelt of baked bread and cake crumbs. Phelim grabbed hold of its greasy wrist—to show he refused to be hustled out of his own home, especially with a mad dog roaming the neighbourhood. The domovoy did not resist. He simply shot the bolt on the door with the other hand, and lifted the latch.

'You are the one,' he said. 'You must go. You must stop the Worm waking. You must save us.'

Phelim snorted with laughter at the ridiculous notion of him saving anyone from anything. But the domovoy's reaction was to hit him—half slap, half punch—with the back of his tarry fingers. There was no more reason to laugh. Phelim realized that it was no longer he who held the domovoy by the wrist; the domovoy held him. With a twist which half wrenched Phelim's arm from its socket, the creature pushed him out through the door and tried to close it again with Phelim on the outside.

His shoes scrabbled on the stone step. He got his fingers round the edge of the door—'Oh no you don't!'—but had to snatch them out again as the glashans herded up and added their weight to the domovoy's, leaning against the door. They could not shoot the bolt for a few seconds, because Phelim was hammering so hard, jolting the door on its hinges. He pounded on it with his shoulder, his forehead, his two fists. But at last the bolt thudded home and the key turned and the invaders dropped back from the door with a communal sigh.

Now Phelim was on the outside of the windows looking in, flattening his nose and cheeks against the glass, whitening his forehead with the pressure, clouding his reflection with shouting, *'Let me in! The Black Dog! Let me in for pity's sake!'* Old paint flaked as he rattled the windows, but the creatures inside the house only gawped back at him, potatoes clutched against their chests, huddling together in the middle of the room.

Phelim stepped back, looking for a way to climb up—get clear of the ground—if the dog came back. He accidentally stepped on a chicken, whose soft, warm, feathery body squelched under his shoe. With a cry of disgust he ran to the coalbunker. He was like the dog now, looking for a way in. He stood panting on the cracked roof-felt, brandishing the coal-shovel for a weapon. *'Open the door, you!'*

The upstairs windows were still open. If he could climb up there . . . Phelim threw the shovel aside with a clang. But just then the domovoy's face appeared at the open window, leaning over the sill. He was holding the pillowcase full of junk. Instead of dropping the whole thing down, he began to take items out one by one, show them to Phelim—'Need plenty luck!'—then drop them on his head. It was enough to

10

stop Phelim getting his balance and, when it came to the horse brasses, enough to make him retreat.

'Let me in! *Please!*' he begged. *'The dog will get me! I don't want to go anywhere!'*

'Only you. You are the one,' said the domovoy implacably. 'You or no one,' and he shut the window, banging it once or twice before the swollen wood wedged back inside the frame. Once more he mouthed through the glass: 'Go.'

There was a wind blowing—a heartbroken, desolate wail of wind. Tears sprang into Phelim's eyes, and he had the oddest feeling that they were nothing to do with being locked out of his home.

2

Mad Sweeney

The people in the house wanted him to go somewhere, do something. But all that interested Phelim Green was safety. He fully expected at any moment the sound of paws on the gravel, and that throaty, rasping bark. If he stayed where he stood, among the slaughtered chickens, he was probably finished. Yes, he would go—but only to fetch some good strong men to shift these glashans out of the house before his sister came home.

There was not a house within miles, but he would find someone to help him.

With a last futile, raging kick at the door, he picked his way through the wreckage of the garden and, heaving open the gate, stepped out into the lane. The cottage windows were crammed with small Neanderthal faces baring their teeth in nervous grins. They pointed at the things on the ground the domovoy had pelted him with—the horse brasses, the rowan, coins, salt, and hot cross buns, as if they wanted him to pick them up.

'You threw them, you pick them up!' he shouted, but his voice sounded weepy and high, so he did not shout any more. He even picked up a bun, remembering that he had not eaten any breakfast, but it was stale as stone, so he just rammed it into his pocket to throw at the dog if it came after him. He picked up all the coins—a threepenny bit and four pennies— thinking how angry Prudence would be if he could not account for them when she got home. Then, hunching his shoulders, he turned his back, hoping to convey the message that he was going for help, that when he came back the

glashans and the domovoy would be sorry, very sorry indeed.

When he saw his sister's horse lying on its side, he thought at first that the Black Dog had killed it. Before Prudence had got big, she had ridden the pony once a week; Phelim's part had been only to groom and feed the beast, but he knew enough to see that it was not lying down out of idleness. As he got closer, he realized with relief that it was not dead, only exhausted. Its coat was caked with dry sweat and there was foam round its mouth. Its eyes rolled in terror as Phelim approached, and it struggled to rise but fell back, breath labouring in its throat, legs twitching. There was a dark oval patch of sweat on its back, with gall marks within it where a saddle had recently been removed. There were whip cuts too on the rump. Someone had been riding the pony in the night.

He went to the stone byre where his sister kept her bicycle. But the bicycle, too, looked as if it had been ridden to destruction. It leaned buckled against the wall, blind of a headlamp, tyres in ribbons, spokes sticking out in as many directions as a porcupine's spines. An oily chain hung down, as from a thing disembowelled. Phelim felt tears prick at the back of his eyes. At least with a bike he could have ridden fast and hard into the wind, shaking off this clammy nightmare, those filthy, unexplained creatures.

Where was the rider who had done this? Still nearby, watching? Refusing to panic, refusing to burst into tears, Phelim walked out of the byre with his thumbs in his belt, trying to keep his shoulders back, to start walking as if it had been his intention all along to walk.

But his skeleton felt unthreaded, his heart overstrained, and before long he stumbled into a clumsy, lumping run, head rolling on his neck, eyes bulging. He ran and ran until the cottage was out of sight, then he sat down on a sawhorse on

13

the edge of the old forestry works and caught his breath.
Which way to go?

Until recently, this roadside clearing had been full of
men—'conchie' pacifists working out the War felling and
sawing timber. He could have asked them for help. But now
the great cape of woodland was deserted, creaking and
sighing, uncrewed. Should Phelim skirt round it or go through
the wood to reach Somerton?

It would be quicker going through the trees, but his sister
Prudence had forbidden him even to play in there, for fear he
lost himself. He wondered why those people he had seen from
the cottage window had been going in the one direction—away
from the town—wondered, too, why he had not gone after
them for help.

Because the Black Dog had gone that way, that was why.

What if it was true—if something was indeed coming,
something worse than the Black Dog?

No, he would cut through Sweeney Woods—put as much
distance between him and the Dog as possible, and reach help
before his sister came back and found the cottage occupied
by prehistoric dwarfs. Prudence frightened him a good deal
more than the intruders; more, even, than the wordless
whispering of the wood.

The cleared forestry roads were wide and bare of vegetation.
But further on, the roads degenerated into a tangle of paths.
Several times, Phelim set off along one, only to find it choked
with nettles or brambles: impassable. He would have expected
to hear more birds than the single woodpecker tapping out its
Morse Code.

Suddenly something big flew overhead and landed in a
nearby ash—something so big that the whole tree was set
bowing and swaying. Phelim saw the shadow on the ground
and thought at once of gorillas. He had seen a gorilla once in a
travelling zoo in Tremadden. He had seen it boxed up in a

14

cage hardly bigger than itself—a vertical slab of black mange, fingers extruding through the close-link mesh, a chest like leather, death in its bloodshot eyes.

Again the shadow passed over him. He caught sight of a foot, a knee, an umbrella spike.

'Where are you going to, my pretty maid? Tell Sweeney! Tell Sweeney!'

He was leaping from tree to tree—prodigious leaps using the springy impulsion of the branches. Sometimes his bare, horny feet seemed to tiptoe across the topmost twigs of smaller trees, but as he landed the leaves engulfed him, gouging at his body, snatching at his matted hair. Phelim ducked down, his arms over his head, thinking he was being bombarded. But it was only the acorns and twigs and seedcases falling on him, dislodged by the leaping man.

'Oh, the Grand Old Duke of York
He had ten thousand men,
He marched them up to the top of the war,
But they won't march down again.'

His yellow skin was stretched tight over the bones of his face, like the skin on custard, and he was painfully thin. As he leapt, he spread his rags of clothes, which were boned or spoked like an umbrella and stretched between arm and leg, catching the wind. He was a pipistrelle of a creature, a flying squirrel, gliding downwards on his outstretched rags only to scramble back into the crown of the next tree and summon up energy for another leap.

'Jack and Jill went up the hill
beyond the Pale to slaughter.
Jack fell down for King and Crown . . . You're Jack, aren't you? Jack o' Green?'

'Phelim,' said the boy determinedly. 'Phee Green. Not Jacko. My father—'

'Well? ''Ever-Good''. That's good, that's good enough,' said

15

the man in the tree and broke off a stick to scratch with under his rags.

'Pardon?'

'Well, every name has meaning, don't it? Yours means "ever-good". So. Ever-good Jack o' Green: you're the man.' And the old man bounded sideways into an elderberry bush, spattering his hands and face with juice. He crouched on a bough, examining his hands. 'Look at that. I'm all blood.

And when they were up, they were up.

And now they are down, they are down . . . '

He sang loudly and cheerfully and very flat. 'You got a task and a half if you're to do it, Green Man. You'll need a Maiden. And a Horse to carry you. I'll be your Fool. But you must needs do it. There's none else. And it's a fair step to Storridge and beyond.'

Phelim stared back the way he had come. Could this old airborne tramp possibly know what had passed between him and the glashans in the living room? Had he swung through the trees all the way from the cottage? Had he been watching?

'Did you ride my sister's bike last night?' he asked accusingly. 'It's wrecked.'

'Not me, not me. Old Sweeney never comes down. Not since he come up . . .

Hey diddle diddle,

the cat's on the griddle,

there's weevils eating the flour.

Napoleon laughs to see such fun . . . Bike? Bike? What's a bike?'

Phelim's sister would definitely have forbidden Phelim to talk to this smelly old derelict. Amazing as his feats of flying were—for he really did appear to fly—his conversation was even wilder than his behaviour, and Prudence did not like wildness, oddities. 'Keep respectable,' she liked to say. 'Trouble can't fasten on you if you keep respectable.'

'She'll say it was me. She'll say it's my fault it's wrecked,' Phelim said reproachfully.

'Hag-ridden, I 'spect,' said Sweeney. 'Hag-ridden last midnight. There were plenty hags out last night. Hatchlings, all of them. They're hatching all the time! The Worm warms as she wakes, see.'

The tramp spoke through a fistful of elderberries. His tongue crushed the fruit against the roof of his toothless mouth, then he spat out a huge clod of pips and skins and stalks. Like an owl voiding pellets of vole and mouse.

'I'll take you there. Thine is the glory, but you need Mad Sweeney to take you, show you the way. Mad Sweeney has the Knowledge, see.' He stretched his yellow, scrawny neck to hold his head erect. 'I have it. It came to me—with the Fear.' Then he shrugged. 'Don't want it. But I have it. I can take you. I know where the Worm lies.' For the first time he looked Phelim in the eye, and there was a belligerent flash of pride. 'I know what they think of me, but they still need Mad Sweeney. Folks still need my Knowledge.'

In Somerton post office Phelim had seen a man like this—a soldier home from the war. Shoppers had walked round him, avoiding him, ignoring his shouted gibberish. Prudence said the shelling had knocked the wits out of him; it happened to lots of men, she said. That did not seem very reprehensible to Phelim, but Prudence had pulled him away from the soldier as if the man's lunacy were a contagious disease. Was Mad Sweeney shell-shocked, too? Somehow he did not look quite like the man in the post office.

'Do they call you Sweeney because you live in Sweeney's Wood?' he asked: as neutral a remark as he could think of, on the spur of the moment.

'They call me mad, because I'm mad,' said Sweeney in a sad voice softer and more musical by far than his singing. Then he brightened. 'Did they really call the wood after me?

17

Well, well. Follow me, Green Man.' And he sprang away—a gibbon's leap across a chain of ground, setting the trees nodding and whispering like the women in Somerton post office.

And Phelim did follow, not because Mad Sweeney had told him to, but because he had realized he was lost. Presumably Sweeney knew a way out of the woods.

'It's a great long way. You'll need an 'orse!' called Sweeney over his shoulder.

Phelim took no notice; he could not ride. Besides, it was not so very far to Somerton—ten miles maximum through the woods, if he remembered rightly the map in Prudence's bureau.

It worried him when the trees petered out and he reached a river. He did not remember a river on the map—not between the cottage and Somerton. As far as he knew, there was only Braide Brook, away to the west. He was just about to query it with Mad Sweeney when he realized that Sweeney was gone. There were no trees, and where there were no trees, Sweeney did not go. Phelim was on his own again.

To his infinite relief, he saw something welcome at last. Two, three, four washing lines, each the length of a ship and filled from end to end with men's washed shirts, billowed, dazzling, along the far bank. He must have reached Somerton already, or stumbled on some little village he had not known existed. Such a number of shirts! There must be a hundred households hereabouts, and each with its full quota of men. That was strange enough in itself, since the War.

Phelim broke into a run, eager to see the first house.

But there were no houses. There was only a single washerwoman, crouching by the ford, her dress hoiked up above her bony knees, her bare feet half submerged in the river's mud. She was washing more shirts—beating them against a large, flat, oval rock, daubing creamy green soap

18

along the collarless neckbands. As Phelim ran towards her, she looked round—a crone's nose like a parrot's beak and cheeks hollow as ashtrays. At first glance Phelim thought she must be holding a second bar of soap in her mouth. Then he saw that her lips were drawn back off her teeth—massive green teeth big as bears' claws.

'This your shirt, laddie?' she asked.

'Well, yes, but I . . . ' There was no mistaking that soft, check flannelette. He had let it out himself with dusting rags, when it got too small for him. Prudence wouldn't buy him a new one—said he was pushing out his chest, pretending the buttons didn't meet—poked him in the ribs to deflate him. He could almost feel the jab now. Phelim put his fingers to his chest, touched the buttons of his soft flannelette shirt. 'No. It's the same as this, but . . . ' Extraordinary, that such another shirt should exist, with the same darns, the same paint stains livid down the front.

'This your shirt, laddie?' called the old washerwoman again.

'No. I mean, it's very like it, but . . . '

The old woman grinned and turned away, slapping the shirt down on to the flat rock beside her, dunking and soaping and scrubbing it into a doughy lump. The mud half burying her feet made them look black and almost webbed . . . The river ran slow at her feet, shallow over the stony ford. From bank to bank, and for several yards upstream and down, the water swirled by, claggy and glutinous from her laundry. Scarlet, too. Dark clots swirled among the brighter red, and even without the hovering flies and the peculiar stench, there was no mistaking it: blood.

He backed away—setting his feet down softly, hoping the old woman would not turn round again and hold up his shirt—that shirt like his—soapy with gore. Finally, he broke into a run, stumbling downstream, knocking into the washing

19

line props, running the gauntlet of a hundred wet, flapping sleeves as he ducked under the lines of washing. Whose were these numberless shirts? Where were their wearers, and what abattoir work did they do that their clothing was so bloody? And why, as the sound pursued him of that small flannelette shirt being smacked down and pummelled against the rock, did he feel blows pounding his chest and arms and back, alternating with a sudden flooding cold which submerged him, stopped the breath in his nose, made him think he was imminently going to die?

3

Alexia

By the time the blowing washing was out of sight, Phelim's throat was rasping dry from running. He lay down on his stomach on the river bank and cupped up water to his mouth. His reflection looked up at him out of the water—hair permanently startled, a white face so spattered with dark freckles that he looked fresh from the trenches himself: splattered by some muddy explosion. His sister's favourite insult came back to him. *'Face like your father, Phee McDirty.'*

'You couldn't have reached the water a while back,' said a voice. 'The river is getting higher every day.'

A girl in a dress of sprig cotton stood on a wooden footbridge over the river. She was about Phelim's age, with upside-down eyes that creased downwards as she smiled; hair white as a dandelion clock. 'There's calamity on the way when the water falls or rises.'

Phelim did not think that a few inches difference in the Braide Brook exactly represented drought or flood on an Egyptian scale. 'Calamity' was rather overstating it. 'Where am I?' he asked. 'I got lost and I need to get somewhere.'

'I know.' The girl was idly pulling flowers off a bunch of weeds in her hand and throwing them on to the river. 'I've been waiting. You were a long time coming.'

His heart sagged. Was she simple, or was she teasing him? He had little to go by, seeing so few children day to day. But Prudence had warned him that most children were not to be trusted. *'They're all mischief like you, Phee McSinner.'*

'I have a problem at home,' he called over to the girl on the bridge. 'I need to get some help.'

'That's me,' said the girl looking at him from under her hand. 'I am Alexia.'

'I don't think you could get the people out of my house. Thanks all the same. Not unless your dad's a policeman.' Phelim rarely met people, and he was shy, but this Alexia wore her eyebrows high and her face pushed slightly forwards, as if eager to listen; that had novelty for Phelim. His sister never wanted to hear anything he had to say. He climbed up on to the bridge, talking as he went.

'It's the domovoy's fault. He asked them all in and then they threw me out—out of my own house, I ask you! And there was this fearful dog outside—ate all the chickens. God's honour! Well, I wasn't waiting: I got out of there! I told them right out. "I'll set the constables on you!" . . . But then the pony was winded and the bike was kaput and I had to walk, so I went through the forest, and there was this man—mad as a loon—leaping about in the trees. Have you seen him? Mad Sweeney? Do you know about him? You're a girl. You ought to watch out. He pretty near flies—God's honour! . . . But I lost him. He ran out of trees. And then there was this woman . . .'

He paused, hearing the nonsense tumble out of him in a babbling torrent, beginning to doubt the truth of it himself. Perhaps he was sick, hallucinating.

'Mad Sweeney? Of course, I know him,' said Alexia. 'It was him told me to meet you here. I'm to be your Maiden. There's no harm in Sweeney.'

'Oh!' Phelim was taken aback. 'He does exist, then?'

'You just told me about him. How could he not exist?'

Phelim ignored this. 'Is he mad enough to wreck a bicycle, would you say?'

'A bicycle?' said Alexia in much the same way that Sweeney had said it. 'How would he use a bicycle in the trees?'

That sank him. Phelim stood silent and awkward, pulling splinters off the bridge rail, wishing he had run downstream instead of up. Alexia was still looking at him brightly, intently. Still, it was a mistake to have told her about the domovoy. 'You must think I'm touched,' he mumbled.

She considered this. 'No. I thought you would be. But you don't seem clever enough. Not like Sweeney. But you shouldn't blame your domovoy, you know. He's very scared. So are the glashans. All those years they've helped people, but what will people do for them? Lock their doors against them and leave them to the Hatchlings.' All her brightness was suddenly eclipsed, and she leaned forward over the rail and dropped her flowers. 'People have forgotten to care about them,' she added, and seemed about to cry.

Phelim felt oppressed. It must be like this to be new-born and pushed about in a perambulator through an incomprehensible world, having larger-than-life strangers forever bending over you, blocking out the sun, talking gibberish. He leaned on the bridge rail alongside Alexia. Lots of things passed Phelim by, living as he did in a remote, rural cottage, all alone with his sister. He did not mind being ignorant. What he did mind was people talking to him as if he *ought* to understand.

Phelim looked down at the river, saw that pallid, freckled reflection of his again. He looked down at the river, then round at the girl beside him. He looked back down at the river—saw himself, saw the bridge's black underside—but no girl beside him. Shooting out a hand sideways, he accidentally poked Alexia in the ear, recoiling as if the ear were red hot.

'You're a ghost,' he said, lacking the breath to speak loud.

'No, I'm not. I'm your Maiden.'

'But—'

'I just don't have a reflection,' said Alexia, as if it were a common affliction. 'Nor a shadow, come to that. So?'

Phelim looked. He moved Alexia out on to the middle of the bridge and searched round her like a dog round a lamppost. His shadow searched with him.

'Please don't worry about it,' she said, nursing her poked ear. 'It really isn't worth worrying about. Not like the water level rising. Still, you can make it all right again, can't you? That's why you're here.'

'Oh, not you too!' He looked up at her from all fours, and noticed that even her little pointy chin did not cast a shadow on her neck. 'I keep saying: there's been a mistake. I'm not who you seem to think I am. I'm *not* this Jacko Green fellow! I'm Phee . . . Anyway, why would I need a girl? What do I want a Maiden for?'

But Phelim did not hear her answer. He had forgotten about shadows and reflections, shirts and madmen.

The slats of the bridge were not edge-to-edge. Through the gaps, he could see running water crumbling the daylight into pieces of brightness—diamonds and zircons and sapphires and topaz. There were red gems, too—carnelian and rubasse—and the sheen of gold metal.

Phelim leaned out so far under the bridge rail that Alexia caught hold of his shirt, thinking he would fall.

'Look! Look at that! There! See?' he shouted. *'Treasure!'*

'No,' said the girl.

How could she deny it? Floating down the river, some on the surface, some just below, somersaulting in the current, were the contents of some mediaeval treasure chest, some Viking plunder or robber's hoard. Chalices and bowls, plates and candlesticks, belts and brooches and clasps were washing downriver, tumbling over and over, splintering sunlight through a hundred inlaid gemstones. Maybe the rising river had unearthed them, washed them out of their hiding place. All he had to do was reach down and grab them, and he would be rich. 'Come on! Quick! Let's get them!' There were coins, too, like shoals of fish—gold and silver and guinea pieces. 'We need a net—something to catch them in!'

Phelim ran off the bridge and splashed into the shallow water, shoes and ankles submerged, trying to reach the things floating past.

'Don't, Jack, don't! Let them go!' Alexia was still on her bridge. He might have taken more notice of her if she had used his proper name.

Phelim splashed deeper in his desperation to catch hold of the treasure. Fortunately some back-eddy in the river seemed to be delaying it, stopping it from washing on by, down to where the washerwoman could get her misshapen, arthritic hands on it all. A jewelled goblet floated tantalizingly close to his outstretched fingertips. 'For pity's sake, help me!' he shouted at the girl.

'No! I won't help you drown yourself! Don't you know *anything*?'

Phelim knew plenty. He knew, for instance, that the world turned on money. His sister had told him that, time past number. Some of the things she blamed him for were unfair, but when she told him he cost her money, how could he deny it? When she told him, 'Without you, I could make ends meet!' there was no arguing. Now he could pay his way! If he could just reach . . . *'What's the matter with you? It's only shallow!'* he shouted at the girl on the bridge.

He waded deeper, till the water reached the tops of his thighs. It was very cold.

Suddenly, just when he was cursing Alexia for being a helpless, gutless, useless girl, she did something extraordinary. She perched herself on the top rail of the bridge and, with a banshee yell, launched herself into the river.

It was a clumsy, uncoordinated dive, all arms and legs flailing, her face screwed up and turned aside from the impact. She landed right in the middle of the treasure, hammered golden bowls bobbing up against her face, coins spinning through her spread fingers. Then she sank.

He expected her to sink and bob up again—the water could not be more than chest-deep. She would put down her feet and stand up, clasping the booty to her chest, passing it to him. Already he thought how marvellous she was to do it.

But Alexia did not come up. And there was no more shine of metal or gems. He waded forwards. Something gripped his ankle and tried to pull it from under him. A geyser of bubbles broke from Alexia's entry point.

Forgetting shadows and gold and reflections, Phelim pushed forwards through the water, which shoved at him like a bully. Hands submerged, he groped about, feeling for the girl's foot or hand or dress. The water around him was full enough of life, but not of sprig cotton. There must be eels—knotting cables of elvers, forests of slimy weed and sharp crayfish. Leeches, even. Slippery suckered tendrils fastened around his wrists and thighs, crawled inside his shirt. Through the surface he saw eyes—not Alexia's green eyes, but eyes with yellow, nictitating lids. There were mouths, too, full of pike-sharp teeth, and jellied masses like frogspawn. His sister's voice clamoured in his head: her favourite question: *'What have you done now, Phee McLummock? What have you done now?'*

'LET HER GO!' screamed Phelim, and plunging his face and arms through the bubbling surface, he looked for Alexia under water.

What he saw, there were no words to describe. How many tentacles, how many eyes, the size and anatomy of his ambusher. But there were no gemstones, that much was certain, no shiny chased metal, no coins. As the angler dangles a worm to fool the fish, the Drac baits its swim with gold and silver, because the Drac fishes for humans.

Feeling a silky cloud of softness brush his knuckles, Phelim grabbed a fistful and yanked. He pushed with his feet off the

26

Drac's stomach, and broke surface, swimming with one arm, his other knotted in Alexia's hair. Twice the monster pulled him back under, but the third time it grabbed his shoe and the shoe came off so that Phelim pulled free and struck out downstream. He dragged Alexia behind him by her hair, like a sea anchor.

'Over here, Green Man! Over here!'

On the far bank, where an oak overhung the river, Mad Sweeney squatted like an orang-utan on a jutting branch, his bony knees to either side of his head. 'Over here, Green Man!'

The bank was pocked with rat and vole holes normally above the waterline but swamped now and under water. The holes made steps for Phelim, though with the added weight of the girl, the holes distorted and collapsed under his feet.

'She's dead. She's dead. She must be dead!' gasped Phelim, ingested water bursting out of his nose as he spoke.

Even when he lay half in, half out of the water, one hand on a tree root, one on the scruff of Alexia's dress, Mad Sweeney kept to his tree and did not come down to help, only shuffled from end to end of the branch like a budgerigar on its perch. Phelim had to drag her out all by himself.

'Pass me up her feet!' said Sweeney when Alexia lay slumped and inert on the bank, her mouth full of potamogeton weed.

Phelim raised Alexia's feet high enough for the man in the tree to grab them, and Sweeney shook her, like someone emptying out a bag. River water and weed, fish fry and noise came gurgling out of her inverted face like beer out of a bottle. Sweeney shook her once or twice more, jerkingly. No shadow jerked on the ground beneath her, but she did begin to cough.

Words bubbled out of her in wet mouthfuls: 'He's a fool, Sweeney! How can he be the one? The boy's a fool!'

'I got you out, didn't I? I jumped in and helped you!'

'*I* am Alexia. *I* should help *you*,' she retorted ungratefully. 'But you don't listen! Why wouldn't you listen? I had to jump in to show you . . . to show you it wasn't how it looked . . . Fool! We can't afford to lose you!' She was flushed with exasperation and coughing. '*You* have to stop the Stoor Worm waking!' She gagged and turned her head away, stomach still slopping with river water.

Phelim shook himself and jumped up and down, trying to get warm. His lost shoe washed up against the bank and he retrieved it. The teeth holes in it were real enough. He said: 'I expect it was a sturgeon fish. I've heard sturgeon sometimes swim up rivers.' There had to be a rational explanation.

But Mad Sweeney had roosted in his oak tree for a midday sleep, and Alexia was busy being sick. It did not seem a good time to tell either of them that they did not really exist.

Perhaps it was not one bad dream he was having, but different ones strung together. He ought to find that out at least. 'I saw a woman earlier,' he said. 'Scary, she was. Feet like a swan, and she was washing all these shirts . . .'

A swirl of damp hair obscured Alexia's face. 'Oh yes, I saw her too,' said Alexia's voice from beneath the hair. 'The Washer-at-the-Ford. Another death in the offing.'

'What?'

'She doesn't worry me specially. People are always dying, aren't they? Old people. Sick people. Soldiers. She must sit there all the time: doing her washing. She doesn't worry me. Just so long as it isn't *my* shirt she's washing, of course!' Alexia gave a sodden, feeble laugh.

Don't you hate dreams like that, thought Phelim. When the fear crawls down you like a sack of tarantulas, and still you can't wake up.

'I think I should be getting home now,' he said, but they ignored him.

28

4

The Reapers

'Best speak soft,' said Sweeney. 'You can be sure the coranieids are listening.'

Like birds moved to sing by the first light of dawn, Sweeney began to speak in the fading afternoon. He had a nervy, twittering voice and, given that he would come down no lower than the lowest branch of a horse chestnut, it was not easy to understand his whispering.

'It was the guns what waked her. Them big guns shook the ground—set the leaves trembling sixty miles off. I thought muskets were loud. I thought thirty-pounders were. But those over yonder—thousands of guns, all hammering away like the Wayland blacksmith at his forge, all day and all night.'

'France, you mean? The War?'

'Mines and mortars,' Sweeney went on. 'Shaking rock into slurry. Rifles firing quick as sticks rattled along a fence. The sky light as day at midnight. Enough to wake the Dead, let alone the living. And the Worm began to wake. All set to sleep away ten thousand year, but no, they had to go waking her with their guns. The sleeper is waking! Her body grows warm. As her body warms, the rocks under her start to hatch. That's what we're seeing: the first of the Hatchlings. First the Hatchlings and then their mother, that's what! That's what has the fright gnawing on me like a million rats! That's what you got to save us from, boy!' His voice rose to a thin, wavering wail. 'Why did they have to go waking her? Bringing the End down on their own heads. And mine. And mine, God save me.'

Phelim glanced across at Alexia, to see if she would wink

and grin, make some sign that Sweeney was rambling mad. But she sat with her knees pressed into the sockets of her eyes. Every so often, a strand of her grey-white hair would come adrift in the wind and blow away, as if her thoughts were travelling to the place Sweeney spoke of, where the Stoor Worm stirred in its sleep.

He would not ask. He did not want to know. He refused to become involved. He would not ask *what* the Stoor Worm was, or what it had to do with him, or what it was hatching. He would not. He would not. He would not. As long as he did not ask, none of this nonsense concerned him.

'When Assipattle fought the Stoor Worm and felled it,' said Sweeney out of his tree, 'the tail thrashed up and down, up and down—parted the lands—split Britain from Norway and Sweden . . . Assipattle stuffed her liver with burning peat—to kill her, see?—but she clenched her body in a ball, and sank into the sea. In her pain she vomited out her teeth: Orkney, Shetland, the Faroes . . . The water springs up hot in Iceland because of that peat still burning inside her. When she shifts herself, the oceans overwash the shores. And when she wakes . . . '

Phelim jumped to his feet and went to the other side of the horse chestnut tree. *'I don't know what you're talking about.* You've got me mixed up with someone else. I don't want to know. It's all hokum you're talking! Fairy stories! Hokum!'

Sweeney's voice pursued him, like a cold draught. Phelim turned up the collar of his flannelette shirt, but it would not cover his ears.

'When she wakes, she'll eat up us all and drink up the sea from here to the Baltic. Maybe three months, maybe three years. Meantime, the rocks under her keep on hatching—more and more—hatching out things as haven't hatched for centuries, things folk have forgotten to fear, things folk don't even *believe in* no more! Hardly a man remembers how to fend them off . . . '

Phelim put his hands over his ears.

'Time was, people paid their tributes—salt, corn, blood. Debts to the Old Magic. Not any more. The tributes have stopped. Folk don't honour their debts. The saints go unblessed; harvest gets taken without a word of thanks. It's like a wall, don't you see it, lad? You got to keep it mended. You got to keep on plugging the holes, or the enemy can get through and at you. Now the Hatchlings are coming, and what's to shield us from them? We've starved our glashans, bricked up our domovoys, forgotten the magics . . . '

Phelim watched the hairs of his arm rise to meet the evening chill. 'These Hatchlings you say are coming . . . ' he called from behind the tree. 'What are they like? I mean what *are* Hatchlings?' A terrible afterthought overtook him. 'Are they like big black dogs?'

'Black Dog, yeah. And bugganes and the dracs and barguests. Picktree Brag, the boas, the triton, the ushteys. The whole nestful! Corn wives, the nuckelavee, the boobrie.' Sweeney banged the side of his head with the heel of one hand, trying to dislodge from the great menagerie of his memory all the beasty names. 'Redcaps! Merrows! Cobbolds! All of them!' He grew fierce, gesticulating and jabbing his forefinger at the tree, in place of Phelim. 'Your grandparents knew! Your great-grandparents! Why didn't they warn you all? They *did* warn you, I'll swear! But people stopped listening. No respect for the old Wisdom. Now the year turns about like a weather vane, any old how, and the glashans aren't fed, and the yew trees are grubbed up, and the witches sniggered into nothingness, and never a piece of iron put up on a door . . . Well, they can all come down on us now, can't they? The Hatchlings!'

Behind his tree, Phelim rocked to and fro, to and fro, trying unsuccessfully to shut out the words. 'Don't tell me! Tell Assipattle! Who's this Assipattle? Why don't you ask him? If he fought it last time he can fight it now! Ask Assipattle, why don't you, but leave me in peace!'

Sweeney's voice came back soft and sinister. 'We might, an' he hadn't been dead these two thousand year.'

The dark forest whispered at Phelim. As dark fell, he wanted to be back by the brightness of the river where the swallows were skimming insects off the surface of the water.

'Tomorrow we'll away to the Anvil and find you an 'orse, Green Man. An 'orse to carry you to the Worm!'

At last Mad Sweeney fell silent. Perhaps he was asleep. Phelim crawled around the trunk to look.

But it was not so. He was just in time to see Sweeney, up on his branch, snatch a swallow out of the air, crack it like a nut against the tree-trunk, and peel open its feathery chest. Feeling inside with a finger, he made a grimace, then discarded the creature with a flick of the wrist which sent it floating off downstream, supper for the pikes. Settling the ribbed bulk of his greatcoat around him like great ungainly wings, the bird-man crooned gently to himself as he licked the blood from his fingers.

' . . . won't you marry me
With your musket, fife, and bell?
Ah no, sweet maid, I canna marry thee,
For I'm dead and gone to hell.'

Phelim cowered back into the shadows. He did not know what frightened him most; the dark of the woods, the wildman, or the words. He would wake early and sneak away—pretend he had never met Alexia or Sweeney, the glashans or the domovoy—pretend he had never seen, in his imagination or out of it, the Washer-at-the-Ford, washing his paint-stained shirt.

Before either Alexia or the madman were awake, Phelim crept away through the forest. He put them behind him like a dream, like a bad dream. He put them out of his mind, along with everything they had said, and by sunrise he scarcely even believed in them.

The land on the far side of the forest was nothing like Phelim's stony valley at home. It was good farmland, with field after field of wheat. Here at last there would be people, ordinary farm workers and housewives, who did not jump from tree to tree or believe in monsters. Besides, trees were few and far between—just may-bushes and elms rising out of ancient stone walls. The day was perfect, too, warm by dawn, bright and clear and red-gold with ripening wheat.

The wheat rippled in such shimmering waves that a cart, moving along a lane between two unreaped fields looked like a boat adrift on sunlit sea.

'Please! Excuse me! *Excuse me!*' Phelim called out. He clambered over a drystone wall and on to the road, startling the horse. 'I need help!' Phelim said urgently. 'I got trouble!' He glanced over his shoulder, half expecting to see Alexia and Sweeney coming after him.

'What kinda trouble, boy? Sickness?' asked the driver of the cart.

'It's people. They've moved in and shut me out—out of my own house!' Phelim explained as best he could, not mentioning the smallness of the intruders, not mentioning that they were naked and brutish, not mentioning domovoys.

'That'll be gypsies,' said the driver sagely, and Phelim did not contradict him.

'Use the world like it belongs to 'em.' He reined in his horse.

Plenty of the reapers in the cart were willing to go and evict the scoundrels from Phelim's cottage, but the one in charge said it would have to wait till the day's harvesting was done. 'Few enough hands left to wag a sickle, as it is. Tell you what, boy. Help out a day, reaping, and we'll come over a'night and turf out your visitors,' he offered.

Phelim liked the idea of wielding a sickle; he had never done it before. 'Tonight would be cracking!' he said. 'I'm sure my sister would give you some cider and supper for your trouble.' He was not sure of any such thing, but reapers and shearers are notoriously thirsty men, and he thought it might save them changing their minds.

So he hopped up on to the tailboard, before the foreman could change his mind. What he had said about the shortage of hands was true: there were relatively few men of working age among the reapers in the cart: mostly schoolboys and old men. The Great War had taken so many. But Phelim did not want to think about the War; that way he would start thinking about the noise of the big guns and the Stoor Worm waking . . . He shook his head to be rid of the Great War—let his eyes trail mesmerically back along the wheel-tracks in the road.

Then he sat up with a start. It might have been his imagination, but just for a moment he thought he could make out, through the clouds of dust churned up by the cart's wheels, a small figure trudging along in their wake; a girl, being left further and further behind as the cart rattled off to harvest.

He had never held a sickle before. They warned him, laughing, to take care of his shins and free hand—not to 'cut himself off at the knees' by mistake. Then they ranged themselves around a field of ripe wheat and their voices were one by one obliterated by the gentle, breathing hiss of the waving crop. Already the day was hot.

The wooden sickle handle blistered Phelim's palm and the blade grew steadily blunter as he hacked inexpertly at the brittle stalks. Reaping was not half so easy as it looked. He wrapped his palm in a dirty handkerchief. The stubble pricked his ankle bones above his shoes—over and over in the same place—and harvest flies infested him like lice. It was horrible work.

Now and then, he heard one reaper call to another, but within the yellow surf of tossing wheat Phelim could see nothing of them. He might as well have fallen overboard from a ship.

The cart was still visible, up on the road, the horse cropping the roadside grass in the shade of an elm tree. After an hour or so, Phelim could see Alexia, too. She was standing up on the buckboard, watching. All morning she just stood there, watching. Shadowless in the hot sun: watching. More than once, he said under his breath, 'Go away, wretched girl. Why don't you just *go*?' But even as he thought it, he could hear his sister's nipping voice: *'Never make a gentleman out of you, Phee McDonkey.'*

In the mid-morning, the reapers emerged, like dusty ghosts, and shared their bottles of lemonade with Phelim. They too had seen Alexia watching.

'Got an admirer, have you, son?' asked the man who had driven the cart. 'Starting early, aren't you?'

'She wants me to do some work for her,' said Phelim, wiping his mouth with his sleeve. 'But she's not paying.'

'Ah!'

'I saw another lass this morning,' said a gangling teenage youth, his face velvety with a first beard. 'What a beauty! Anyone else see her? White frock. Dazzler! Walking in amidst the crop.'

'Damn fool place to walk when sickles are out,' muttered the foreman.

Phelim felt almost adult, sitting with this brotherhood of sweating, mahogany-brown men, discussing girls. Unfortunately, some of the reapers were much younger than he, and plainly flagging less in the heat. They went back to work far more willingly than Phelim did.

Towards noon he thought he heard a different kind of shout. He looked towards the cart. Alexia was beckoning him, her arms flailing round in great loops as though she were dragging the air into sheaves. He was dog tired; he needed to sit down and rest his aching back, his blistered hands, but he refused to give in to her. He turned his back and went towards a different stand of wheat—would have whistled a nonchalant song as he went, but his lips were too dusty.

He had to step over the teenage boy who had talked of a pretty girl in white. Must be taking a midday nap, thought Phelim—except that he was lying so awkwardly, his chest flat to the ground, his face turned back over his shoulder. How could he sleep like that: chest-down, face-up?

Phelim swung his sickle. The wheat hissed, the bearded ears fell against his face making him close his eyes. Then the curve of the blade clanged against something hollow and metallic and black.

A woman's rib cage.

No white-clothed beauty, this. At close quarters, he could see the rust-red eyes, the adze-shaped chin, the nose as curved as a bill-hook. Her long, black skirt was pale with dust, but not the shiny black of her iron upper body. Her long, flue-black, iron breasts had blunted countless sickle blades as she stood amid the wheat, waiting for her victims to blunder into her. She held a long-handled scythe, but she and her sisters had not come to harvest wheat.

Only the reapers.

Phelim leapt back—tripped over the yielding softness of the sleeping reaper, and fell over backwards. If he had not, the black blade arcing towards his spine would have sliced him off at the waist. The stubble jabbed into his thighs and elbows as he wriggled out of reach and wormed his way into the uncut corn. Perhaps if he held very still . . . *Snicker-snack! Snicker-snack!* Lopped ears rained down on him. A dark shape

36

prowling close-by gave a sharp, ripping bark. Phelim pushed his way onwards, flat on his belly, pushing with the toes of his boots, scraping over the stony ground, setting the wheat waving . . .

So. It had been a true portent. The Washer-at-the-Ford had held up his own shirt to him; she had known he was about to die—here in this field, like this, among strangers, a winter away from his twelfth birthday, hacked to death by iron reapers!

Grinsch, grinsch: something heavy was pushing its way through the corn, rattling and groaning and smashing the seeds from the ears like spray off the crests of waves. Lying flat along the ground he saw its shadow block out the sunlight as it rolled over him . . .

'Phelim! Phelim Green! Where are you?'

Alexia had picked up the reins and driven the cart out across the field. She drove straight over him, without knowing it, and the great metal-rimmed wheels sank into the earth a whisker from his skull, a hair's-breadth from his clenched fist. He grabbed hold of a bulging metal staple in the tailboard and let the cart drag him out of the wheat. Then he let go, jumped to his feet, and leapt aboard. The look she flung him was a mixture of fright, reproach, gladness, and anger.

Raised up those five or six feet off the ground, Phelim had a much clearer view of the field. He could see how the circular assault of the reapers had shaved a great stubbly tonsure as they worked towards the centre. He could see their bent backs here and there, stained to the colour of wheat by the flying dust. Cat's-paw ripples of wheat marked where some were still working, ignorant of the danger. But whereas before the field had looked like one tossing, golden, unpolluted sea, now there were other, darker shapes. Phelim heard the tinny rasp of a sickle blade striking metal, then an oath. There was an army advancing through the field! Nothing less described it. A

37

hundred corn wives were sweeping through the crop, whisking their scythes at the napes of unprotected necks, at bent and vulnerable backs, at running legs, at arms held up in token of surrender. Their male cousins were with them, too, dog-headed, with iron teeth and claws with which they bit through or notched the last silver sickles raised in self defence by the terrified reapers.

'Faster! Faster!' he shouted at Alexia. 'Get us out of here!'

'What did you think you were doing?' she reproached him. 'We told you! No time to waste! Hatchlings! See? See?' The cart lurched drunkenly over the dry, furrowed ground, towards the road. But they approached the gate diagonally and one of the wheels collided with the gatepost, jolting them to a standstill. 'Unfasten the traces!' said Alexia. 'We'll just take the horse!'

Black and numberless as rooks descending on corn, the corn wives were also moving en masse towards the road. As Phelim fumbled with the buckles of the harness, he thought it might be quicker on foot, quicker just to run. When, from behind, a girl's hand was laid on his head, he turned round, saying, 'Let's just run for it!'

But it was not Alexia. It was the lovely girl in white—it had to be. The youth had not exaggerated; she was beautiful. 'Look, you have to get away from here,' he began warning her, pointing back into the field. But her dusty fingers closed in Phelim's dustier hair and she began to turn his head—twist it—turn his chin round over his shoulder as though his head were the handle of a tap.

His throat was instantly closed up: he could not cry out. He knew his neck was about to snap. He swung at her with his sickle, but the blade passed clean through her and scraped his own left arm. Out of the corner of his eye, the thought he saw his own blood splash red on her white dress . . .

Then she blew away like smoke.

38

The traces fell to the ground; the harness chains rattled loose. Alexia—up on the horse's back now—slapped the reins against its rump. It moved with lumbering slowness, clip-clopping sedately out on to the road while the corn wives began to scramble agilely over the drystone wall. Their iron chests rasped against the upright ridge-stones. A section of wall collapsed under their eagerness.

The withers of the big carthorse were as tall as the wall. All Phelim had to do was climb the open five-bar gate, step across the animal's back and thump down on to the seat of his pants. In front of him Alexia rolled and pitched in her effort to thump her heels into its massive flanks.

'Did you see her? Was she there? She wasn't! It wasn't real!' said Phelim of the girl in white (though the pain in his scalp and neck and arm felt horribly real). 'None of this is real!'

'Your blood fell on her,' said Alexia curtly. 'Otherwise she would have twisted your head round till your brains scrambled. She's the Noonday Twister.'

The horse moved off, swaying, unhurried, placing its big feet carefully between the stones on the earth road. Its warmth and its sweet, rich smell engulfed them. Perhaps the smell of the horse masked their own scent and deterred the dog-headed reapers. Or perhaps they and the corn wives were more intent on their cross-country migration than in chasing a pair of skinny children. The hags swarmed like black beetles across the road and on into the next field. The half-reaped field lay quiet again, the undulating uncut wheat concealing its litter of massacred reapers.

They rode along the road for a long while in silence. Phelim squinted up at the sun and worked out that they were going west—presumably towards their rendezvous with the Stoor Worm. He did not so much as think of objecting.

'Why me?' was the first thing he said. 'Why does it have to be me?'

'You're Jack o' Green. That's who's needed,' she said opaquely.

'But I'm not! I'm not Jacko Green. I'm *Phelim* Green. You're wrong! There's nothing odd about me. Nothing. It's all a terrible mistake.'

She glanced round at him long-sufferingly. 'You saw your glashans, didn't you? The ones who look after your land? You spoke to your domovoy, didn't you? The one who looks after your house? You saw Black Dog and your blood dissolved the Noonday Twister? What more do you want? A mark on your forehead? You *are* Jack o' Green.'

Again he fell silent. The horse swayed soothingly, in time with alternate heart beats. 'What is it you all want me to do?'

'We don't know. We thought *you* would know. We thought you'd be bigger. Stronger. Older. We thought at least you'd be game for the fight—not run off like that.' She sat forward so as not to let her body rest against his. She was plainly disgusted with him. 'Didn't your *mother* tell you it was your duty to come? Or your father?'

'My mother died when I was little! And my father . . . well, he isn't around either. And besides, you got it wrong. I tried to tell you, but you wouldn't listen. I can't do anything! Ask my sister! I'm nothing! I'm nobody! I've got a reflection and a shadow and everything in its right place. I can't fly. You and Sweeney are miles more magic than me! Why can't *you* do it?'

She relented a little, easing backwards into the saddle, her hair brushing his face. 'I'm sorry. I'm sorry about your parents. We'll go along with you, of course we will. I'll be your Maiden. Sweeney will be your Fool. But it has to be you. It has to. Even if you can't do it, you have to try! Sometimes I think the glashans are lucky. They only live in the Now. No past. No future. They get scared, but they don't say, ''I wonder how it will be. I wonder how it will end.'' Me, I can't stop hardly.'

Phelim thought back to his sister's little cottage, the domovoy from behind the stove speaking to him in the present tense: *'Now there is only you.'* Presumably by now the domovoy and the naked potato-eaters would have forgotten Phelim's very existence, unable to hold it in their primitive memories. Only their fear would persist—an intuition of Evil. An ever-present dread of Something Coming.

'When shall we meet up with Sweeney?' he asked.

'Somewhere. When there are trees again. You can never tell with Sweeney. He said I was to take you to the Anvil to get you a Horse—*when I'd caught up with you,* that is.'

'But we have a horse,' he pointed out, ignoring the sarcasm.

'What? This old nag? Well, you could be right, I suppose. It's a horse. But Sweeney told me to take you to the Anvil, so that's where we'll go. I don't know what else to do.'

Phelim understood that feeling well enough. He was accustomed to doing what he was told. In the absence of his sister's nagging shriek and sharp little slaps, he might as well do what this girl told him. He had tried striking off on his own, and look where it had got him. 'Are they really dead? All those men? Back there?' he asked Alexia. 'It's not a vision? I didn't dream it?'

She gave the briefest jerk of her head. 'If we don't go faster than this, every field and every town will be the same inside a month. And worse things than corn wives. The stones are hatching, didn't we tell you? The stones under the Worm . . . '

The carthorse plodded on as slowly as the sun crossing the sky, a ship travelling against the tide. Alexia drummed her heels but it only made her heels sore. 'Oh for a fast horse!' she said, sufficiently loud for the birds to fly up out of a blackberry bush.

Nearby, on the crest of a barrow—an ancient earthwork welling roundly out of the agricultural land—small figures baffled the air with huge butterfly nets of such gauzy thinness that they were not visible from the road below. With slow, figure-of-eight flourishes, the coranieids were sifting *words* from the rising air: tiny whispers no bigger than a pin head, louder oaths black and buzzing as horseflies. Plucking them from the fine-weave mesh, the coranieids transferred them to Kilner jars, sorting and discarding with infinite patience, now and then holding up a jar to their long-lobed ears and shaking the words back into a decipherable hum. ' . . . the Anvil,' they heard, and 'Horse'.

5

Well-Wishers

The matter of the shirt grew in Phelim's imagination with each passing mile. If all these horrors were real, then the Washer-at-the-Ford had been real too. He wanted to grab Alexia by her skinny shoulders and shake her and say, 'It was *my* shirt she held up! My shirt! Do I have to die? Couldn't it mean something else? How can I unsee it?'

But he did not say a word. Alexia was pinning her hopes on him. If Jack o' Green died, seemingly nothing could save humankind from the Stoor Worm's brood of Hatchlings. And the more he thought about that, the more he despaired. After all, he already *knew* their journey was futile. He was going to get killed. He was travelling towards his own death. And yet he kept on going. Why? It must have been like that for the soldiers in the trenches, he thought. Plain common sense and logic told them they would die if they went one more time into no-man's land. And yet they knew they would go. The only taboo was to speak of it, to admit to the fear. The brain inside his head contracted and swelled at the thought of it, making colours flash behind his eyes.

He could not even confide the ghastliness of it to this girl. He had to keep the knowledge locked up, however much it battered on his skull, tried to squirm out through the dry passageway of his throat. If he shared his fears, Alexia would feel the same despair as him. She might abandon him, too, and run off—put a safe distance between herself and the doomed shirt-wearer.

Even if Phelim tore the shirt in shreds, the Washer-at-the-Ford would still be holding its ghostly replica, beating it threadbare on her bloody rock, washing his life out through the fibres. No, there was no way round it. If any of it was true, all of it was true. Phelim was going to die.

Fields gave way to oddly distorted hills—barrow-mounds, perhaps, absorbed into the landscape over three and four thousand years. The road they were on was very straight—a Roman road, maybe, kept free of weeds by centuries of tramping feet. In the distance they could see, scrawled in white chalk on a green hillside, simplified into a few cursive shapes, the symbol of a horse. 'Nearly there,' said Alexia.

The wind began to keen again. Under a cloudless sky, the sound of a winter wind howled and whistled so loudly that they both shivered convulsively.

All at once the temperature dropped, too—not with nightfall nor whipped away by wind, but as if they had stepped in at the door of an icehouse. The carthorse twirled its ears. Its hide began to flicker, and it came to a halt of its own accord, cribbing and sidling and stamping.

In front of them lay a barricade of snow. Right across the road lay a snowdrift so high that the road beyond it was completely obscured. Small summer birds had flown down to investigate the strange whiteness and their claws had frozen to the ice, so that the drift was peppered now with small feathery bundles. Alexia screwed up her face against the wind.

'Snow, in August? Is it a roadblock? An ambush?' said Phelim. They glanced nervously to either side of the road, but saw nothing except that there was no way past, no way of skirting the snowdrift which filled the dip between two steep slopes of loose, grey shale.

Though runnels of meltwater glistened and trickled down it, the drift grew no smaller while they stood there. In fact it seemed to Phelim that the drift was not so much melting as weeping. The soughing, windy sobs appeared now to come from right *under* the mound. He suggested to Alexia that something might be trapped there—had to shout it, because she had her hands clapped hard over her ears.

'Do *you* want to dig it out?' she retorted without unplugging her ears.

He had to agree, he didn't, but she sounded heartless in the face of those lamentations. Surely she must pity anyone driven to weep like that?

I shouldn't stop here and reason this out, he found himself thinking. Instinct. I should trust to instinct. Unfortunately, instinct told him to cry. His throat engorged with tears; his sinuses ached. Sadness was hollowing out his stomach, making him weak . . .

'I think we should get away from here,' he said with the last of his resolve, and nudged Alexia rather harder than he had meant. Her arms flailed as she rolled sideways off the horse. Phelim too jumped down. He began to run. They would have to abandon the horse and find a route on foot over the shale hills.

He said as much to Alexia and, when she did not answer, looked round: she was not behind him. She was still standing at the foot of the snowdrift, shoulders bent, head down, her whole body shaken by sobs. In falling from the horse, she had inadvertently uncovered her ears.

Phelim thought of Odysseus and the Sirens, the voices-which-must-not-be-listened-to. Running back, he grabbed her by the hand, roaring at the top of his voice the first song which came to mind: '*Land of Hope and Glory, Mother of the Free* . . . ' Alexia sniffed, and trailed feebly behind him, her face turned back towards the drift. The wind howled louder, more sorrowfully than ever.

'*How shall I extol thee, Who was born of thee?*

Wider still and wider . . . ' bellowed Phelim. His sister forbade him ever to sing—'*None of your caterwauling, Phee McCrow*'—

but Prudence was not here to hear him, and the racket served to drown out the wind.

'God who made thee mighty . . . '

Alexia joined in with him: ***'Make thee mightier yet!'***

After scrambling up and sliding back down for half an hour over a morass of grey stone, the children found themselves a mile from the road and picking their way between little cairns of sheep droppings. The wind had stopped its soughing. Which way now? They had no idea. However hard they tried to get back to the road, some mine working or slate quarry or awkward shoulder of rock would defeat them, until they could no longer even judge where they were in relation to the road. Instead, they rambled aimlessly cross-country.

Alexia continued to weep, even though the wailing of the snowdrift was long since out of earshot. It was as if some seal inside her had been broken by shaking, and now she could not stop. Phelim did bird impressions and whistled snatches of music-hall songs to try and cheer her up. But it was only the sight of the white horse on the slope ahead of him that was capable of making her smile.

'Do you have any money?' she asked suddenly. It sounded urgent.

Phelim shrugged. 'I never got paid for the reaping.'

'Yes, but do you have any money anyway?'

'Money?' He patted at his trouser pockets and pulled out the threepenny bit and four pennies the domovoy had thrown at him. Prudence would skin him if he spent it.

Alexia looked forlornly at the coins, like a fortune teller thwarted by a smooth palm. 'That's all you've got? That won't buy us much.'

He laughed. 'This isn't mine. I have to give it back to my sister.'

'You mean to say your sister would begrudge you sevenpence?'

46

Phelim considered this. Almost the last conversation he had with Prudence, before she left with her monthly parcel for Oakington, was about the squares of torn up newspaper in the privy—how he used far more than he needed to; how he was an extravagant waster, and took more out of the world than he put into it; how he would be the beggaring of her with his mindless squandering. But he did not say any of this to Alexia: he did not want her to know his faults. Anyway, it was rude to mention toilets, especially to a girl. Instead he said, 'You have to understand: she's much older than me. Twice my age. She has a lot of worries, running the house. We don't have much to spare. Since Dad went off.'

'Off where?'

'Oh. Just "off".'

'We'll have to go back, then,' said Alexia. 'I saw a place. About a mile back. We need silver to get you a horse.' She sounded irritable, as if he should have known.

'I *would* have had sixpence for the reaping,' he called apologetically, as she set off leaving him standing. But he could hear his sister, even as he said it: *'Always the big excuse with you, Phee McHopeless.'*

Alexia led the way back, through two miles of oak and ash trees, to a low, square, brick construction. Phelim thought at first it was a lambing fold until he saw the rope emerging over the wall, secured figure-of-eight fashion round a metal cleat. It was a well.

Phelim hauled on the rope and raised up a pail of water floating with moss. He offered it to Alexia, then drank, himself, though it was difficult to lift the heavy oak bucket and he slopped it all down his front. Alexia took it out of his hands but still held it out towards him.

'No, thank you. No more.'

Without warning, she grabbed Phelim's wrist and banged it sharply on the bucket, so that his precious pennies plopped

47

into the bucket. Then it was gone again, down the well, the rope snaking and fraying its way through the groove in the well's coping.

'What did you do that for?' SPLASH went the heavy bucket into the water below. Phelim complained, loud enough for any listening coranieids to catch: 'You threw my money down the well!'

'Yes. Now we have to gather acorns,' said Alexia. 'All you can find. Use your shirt. I don't know how many it takes.'

Acorns. Acorns. Acorns. Collecting acorns becomes an end in itself after a while. Fistfuls and scores of acorns. In among the oak trees they lay about like tiny green eggs in their brown egg cups. Phelim scurried about bent double, reaching through nettles and brambles to pick them up. Large birds or small animals crashed about in the undergrowth, but Phelim and Alexia took no notice, working on till their fingernails were black with leaf mould, their backs aching. The only difference between them was that Alexia knew why she was doing it, and Phelim did not.

When Alexia's skirts were full, and Phelim's shirt was bulging with forest mast, they ran back, with a funny, waddling gait, to the well, where they emptied their takings over the wall. They fed the open mouth of the well like thrushes feeding a gaping cuckoo chick. They had no notion at all of the well's appetite for acorns.

'Why are we doing this?' panted Phelim as they raced each other back to the oak wood. 'What are they for?'

'Silver, of course!' she gasped, shaking the stems and mess off her sprig cotton. 'Don't you know anything? If we feed it enough, the well will turn your coins to silver! To buy you a horse!'

Turn copper into silver? It sounded absurd. But Alexia was, after all, a witch—halfway to being a witch—and she knew things. If wells could do that! Phelim was suddenly much more in favour of magic. If wells could do that, then Alexia and he could mint money enough to buy Wales and rig it overall in flags and pennants and sail it away over the edge of the world. Silver? That was one word Phelim had always known the magic of.

When they got back to the well a second time, Alexia emptied her skirts and Phelim (with a furtive glance out of the corner of his eye) shipped his shirt too into the well's yawning mouth. He made it look like an accident.

'Oh! Your shirt!' cried Alexia reaching out, but she was too late. It fluttered its sleeves as it fell out of sight into the dark.

'Never mind,' said Phelim. 'I can always buy a new one, if there's silver.'

It took both of them to haul up the oak bucket. Would the coins have fallen out of it as it filled with water? Had the children fed the well with enough acorns to earn its thanks, or did it demand the harvest of a thousand forest acres? *Bang bang*, the bucket scraped up the mossy wall, slopping water back down into the dark. It almost overbalanced as they stood it on the wall.

Both children bent their heads to drink, like horses, from the pail. Running had made them thirsty, and their stomachs were cramping for want of food. Besides, they dared not look straight away, to see if Phelim's sevenpence was still there.

Above them, the sun went in. The dazzling died off the surface of the bucket, and they could see to the bottom. There lay six silver florins. Only one bun-penny remained, still bearing the head of Queen Victoria, tight-lipped and unamused, still obstinately copper.

'We're rich!' said Phelim.

He could scarcely credit that a world which had once known this manner of trick had, through lack of interest, forgotten how to do it, forgotten it was even possible! To feed acorns to a well and get silver in return? Why was the world not full of rich men and bare of oaks?

With difficulty he squeezed the coins into the pockets of his ill-fitting, too-small, embarrassingly short trousers. He would buy himself some new ones in the first town they came to. The war was over, and it was no longer illegal for a boy of his age to wear *long* trousers. He would buy—

'Oh look, Jack! Your shirt!' cried Alexia delightedly. A nail protruding from the bucket had snagged Phelim's shirt and brought it up, wet and drooping, into the light of day. She disentangled it, wrung it out and offered to carry it till it dried. But he took it from her and put it on, wet.

So. There was to be no shucking off his fate—no slithering out of it like a snake shedding its skin. The shirt clung clammy. The well had returned his fear to him as surely as a dog fetching back a stick.

The silver coins in Phelim's trouser pocket still pressed into his groin, but somehow now, they were not worth quite as much as before. And when he looked up and saw the nuckelavee scratching and snuffling up out of the wood, Phelim would have given all the silver in the world to be safely home in bed.

It had no hide—no skin—so that the whole workings of its insides were on constant view—a laboratory of soft fermenting flasks and transparent pipes, membranous valves and seven swilling stomachs. Within its translucent white skull, the working of its spongy brain flickered dimly.

Even though it had no legs, it was large as a bull elephant, crutching itself along on its long bone-and-muscle arms— pull, lift, drag, sprawl. Horns and hoofs and vertebrae were clearly visible inside the churning turmoil of its guts. There were boots in there, too, and absurdly but quite distinctly a wheelbarrow. The nuckelavee regarded the children with its lidless eyeballs.

50

'Down the well!' said Alexia.

It seemed a suicidal thing to do, but they did it, stepping out over the darkness, jamming a foot a-piece into the bucket, and holding their own weight by gripping the lifting-rope. The pulley groaned, and brick dust fell away from its mounting. The rope slid, burning their hands as they lowered themselves down into the dank dark. The circle of daylight above them diminished to the size of a jam-jar lid, then their feet, ankles, knees were awash in icy black water, and their strength was all gone for holding on.

6

A Horse! A Horse!

'There's a ledge!' said Phelim. 'There's a ledge. Can you reach it?'

They clung to the rim of crumbling masonry, keeping themselves afloat, though their feeling feet found no trace of the well's bottom.

The dim flickering of the nuckelavee's brain dipped down into the darkness above them, but though it grunted and strained, its bulk was too great to squeeze down the well. Slowly it ingested the rope; like a strand of spaghetti it snaked away up the well-shaft, the bucket banging against all four walls, dislodging brick dust on the children beneath. They could hear the beast crutching itself around and around and around the well. From time to time, that translucent head, like fairy lights crammed into a Chinese lantern, swayed into sight.

'Don't let it breathe on you!' gasped Alexia. 'It spreads plague!'

The Plague? A mediaeval, brimstone-and-lime terror infected Phelim at the mention of plague. He tried to turn his face away, but there was nowhere to turn it but downwards into the water. Was this, then, to be the fulfilment of the washerwoman's omen: this skin-naked monster dragging its lights and liver over his last remaining footprints, while down below it he drowned? The sapphire blue circle of sky was as beautiful and unreachable as Heaven to the Damned.

In his panic, Phelim lost track of time. He thought about Sweeney and the terror which had made him fly. Far from despising the man, he found himself envying him, for Phelim's fear gave him no power to jump up high, no Knowledge which enabled him to see a way out.

'Will Sweeney be angry with me for creeping off—for not wanting to go on this journey?' he said into the darkness.

'Hardly. He understands about people being afraid.' Alexia's voice came back corrugated with cold. 'It's true, we were expecting you to know about the Stoor Worm—what to do about it. But why should you, if no one ever told you before who you were? First we'll get you your Horse, then we'll head for the sea—for Stoor Head, other side of Storridge. That's the Worm. That's where the Worm is.'

'You know that? Have you ever been there?'

'Oh yes,' she said. He could not believe how off-handedly she said it. 'I used to go there often when I was small. To my Uncle Murdo's place. Far side of Storridge. He used to point it out to me and tell me the story. Of Assipattle, you know?'

'You've *seen* the Stoor Worm? You've actually *seen* it?'

'It's not like you think—not a George-and-the-dragon kind of worm. I can't explain. You need to see it for yourself . . . Uncle Murdo's a great man for the Old Ways. He might have some ideas for you—how to get up close. How to kill it. But Sweeney will find us before then. He'll know. Or something will come to you. How to kill it, I mean. You'll think of a way. You're Jack o' Green, after all.'

Her foolishness was almost enough to make him laugh. 'You're as mad as he is! Listen to you! Here we are, a great gherkin-jar of a monster watching us drown down a well without a rope . . . No one around for miles. How in the name of . . . How the . . . *Just how do you think we're going to get out of here?*'

'Up the rungs, of course.' She shook her head so that her white hair—faintly luminous, like the nuckelavee—spattered him with water. She reached up and took hold of a rusty iron rung set into the wall above her. 'There are always rungs.

53

How else could the farmers get animals out that fall in or re-point the walls or anything. Come on. The nuckelavee will be gone by now. It needs to eat often. It will have gone looking for a sheep or a cow.' Shortly after she cleared the water, the trickles from her clothing pouring down into Phelim's upturned face, she stopped for a moment and shuddered violently. 'Oof,' she said lightly. 'Someone just walked over my grave. I don't like ladders. I never liked ladders much.'

The ground sloped uphill—steeper and steeper uphill, so that soon they were scrambling up on all-fours, dislodging pieces of loose chalk. Then the bracken gave way to grass, and the grass to a grassy baldness, and they found themselves clambering over the very limbs and trunk of the chalk horse they had seen at a distance. At the summit of the hill, they stood up. On the other side, the slope plummeted down into the deep hollow, such as a waterfall carves out at its foot, where hawks were hovering, keeping watch for mice and voles.

Looking back the way they had come, the countryside lay so perfectly still that there was no believing in the nuckelavee, Black Dog, or the corn wives: bad dreams dispelled by waking.

'Whistle,' gasped Alexia, resting her hands on her knees.

'Whistle? Can't . . . even . . . breathe!' panted Phelim.

Then a rabbit made a run for its burrow, and seeing it out of the corner of his eye, Phelim took it for a Hatchling, started, missed his footing, and went tumbling down towards the gully: over and over and over. His shirt tore at the armpits, his tight little trousers split. The six silver florins went spinning out into empty air.

Winded, he lay on his back amid nettles and dock-leaves. The sky overhead flushed several different colours, and the hill reeled. He could just see Alexia's head jutting out over a ledge. 'Now *whistle*, will you?'

Phelim stuck his tongue out at her. He could not whistle. He did not want to whistle. He did not even think it was a good *idea* to whistle and alert those foul Hatchlings to where he was. No, as the wind came back into his chest and the sky turned back to blue, he decided just to lie very still and ignore Alexia in the hope that she and they and everyone would go away and leave him alone for the rest of his short life.

At nightfall all the heat went out of the day and the dewfall made their clothes wet. They had nothing to eat but blackberries gathered from the brambles round about—had tried to eat the hot cross bun from Phelim's kitchen, but found it iron-stale.

Alexia had climbed down to join Phelim in the hollow, and they had whistled until their lips were numb, but nothing had come of it.

'I suppose it's because we don't have the silver any more,' said Alexia accusingly. It was futile to look for the dropped money, though they had tried for a whole hour.

'Nothing to do with it,' he said. 'I *told* you. I'm *not* Jacko Green. I'm nobody. I don't *need* a horse, because I'm not *going* anywhere. There's no point.'

'Nobody says they're nobody,' mused Alexia (clearly troubled in case he was right). 'Everybody's somebody. Most people think they're Everybody. Not you.'

But he only looked at her blankly; the words made no sense to him. 'Tomorrow,' he said, 'why don't we find somewhere with cheese and potatoes and corned-beef fritters, and eat and eat . . .'

'Because you dropped the money.'

'I still got one!' He opened a palm black from holding the one florin-piece tightly all the way from the well.

'Well, whyever didn't you say so? So we do have silver!' exclaimed Alexia. Her frown of mystification returned. 'So why . . . ? Perhaps we're sitting in the wrong place!'

Phelim gave an exasperated gasp and turned his back on her, rolling himself up into a ball against the promise of a long, cold night. They would have to sleep on the Anvil, now, with coranieids and nuckelavees all around. And in the morning, worst of all, *she* would still be there, nagging him about the Stoor Worm and the stones hatching and refusing to believe that she had made a simple, straightforward mistake.

'Don't need a Maiden, either, come to that,' he muttered, but not loud enough for her to hear. His sister had terrorized all but the tamest rudeness out of him.

Alexia sat up for a while longer, hugging her knees, watching the night press in against the hill like a besieging army. Her pale hair shed a strand or two which blew across and clung to his shirt. 'Why not cake?' was all she ventured in the way of conversation.

'What?'

'Why potatoes and cheese and corned-beef? Don't you like cake and ice cream?'

'Not allowed,' murmured Phelim. He was almost asleep. 'Cakes are for Prudence. And I never tasted ice cream. I might not like it.'

During the night, Phelim dreamed of Black Dog. But when he woke, it was worse. Not one dog but forty and more ran yelping and panting past, somewhere nearby. He rose on to his hands and knees, eyes straining against the darkness, dizzy with sleep but as wide awake as if his brain had been dropped in a bucket of acid. The cold sweat from his back passed through his clothes to mix with the damp from the ground. He could not have got to his feet if he had wanted, but crawled through brambles and seven kinds of unspeakable mould on hands and knees away from the noise. He almost put his hand down on Alexia's face.

As she sat up, he put his arm round her. It was a boy's job to look after a girl, after all. 'It's all right,' he said soothing her, patting her shoulder, while his teeth chattered with fright. 'Don't fret. If they come any closer, we'll find a tree, see? Climb up. We'll be quite safe. You mustn't be scared.'

Alexia neither struggled nor shrank up against him. Her teeth were not chattering. 'What can you hear, Phelim?' she asked.

'Geese. I expect it's just geese,' he said. 'Migrating. Geese can make a lot of noise.'

The yelping was almost on top of them now—the deafening, bloodcurdling, unmistakable baying of a hunting pack on the scent of its prey. Phelim curled himself into a ball, arms clamped over his head, spine crackling at being coiled so tight. To cover the noise of the dogs he howled a single desolate note, almost like a dog himself.

'I think you are hearing the Gabriel Hounds,' Alexia said, stroking his hair in gentle, regular little strokes, patting his curled back. 'That proves it. You are a chime child.'

Phelim emerged like a mole from its burrow. 'A what?'

'Born while the clock struck midnight. It means you can hear the Gabriel Hounds hunting the souls of the Damned across the sky.' She said it as if it were a matter of green fingers in the garden, or cold hands for the making of pastry. 'You can hear the Hounds. And talk to the Fairies.'

'You didn't hear them?' said Phelim open-mouthed. 'You didn't see anything?'

Alexia smiled and shook her head. 'I was awake every minute and I didn't see a thing. Well, I saw the soul-mouse creep out of your mouth. So I knew you were dreaming. I saw it creep back in when you stopped. I couldn't bed down till it went back inside, in case it came to any harm: people die if their soul-mouse dies while it's—'

'*I didn't dream those dogs!*' he insisted furiously.

'No. No, I know. But I didn't hear them. I'm not a chime child, you see.' She was infinitely sympathetic, infinitely understanding, infinitely infuriating. 'At least we know now for sure you're the man for the job, Ever-Good Green. You're the one. Now go back to sleep. It's a fair long way to Storridge.'

Phelim woke first and sat watching the dew well up like tears on the flat blades of grass. Plucking a blade, he held it between his two thumbs, to see if he could still produce a squawk. No sound came. He threw the blade away, picked another and blew, feeling the grass rattle between his fingers, startling Alexia awake with a noise like a strangled duck. 'Sorry,' he said. 'I didn't know it would come out so loud.'

At first he thought the ringing thuds were the blows of woodsmen working in the forest. Then he saw the horse galloping towards him, white head tossing, raising a silver spray of dew off the grass: riderless but wearing a saddle, even so.

It was a magnificent piece of horseflesh, so tall Phelim did not even consider he would be able to get astride its back. Its silvery coat was tinged with blue and its mane waved luxuriantly to its knees. The noise which filled its flared nostrils was like the hissing in a seashell: a sea sound. But was there not something strange about its feet? Shouldn't the round part of the hoof face to the front? Perhaps if he did manage to get aboard, the horse would take off backwards at fifty miles an hour.

'Maybe it threw its rider,' he suggested lamely.

'You whistled, didn't you? And it came, didn't it?' But she

drew close to Phelim's side, awed by the magnificence of the creature. It was surely too beautiful to be malign. But she added, 'I'm not sure . . . '

'Never look a gift-horse in the mouth,' suggested Phelim with a nervous snicker. But he kept thinking, too, of the wooden horse of Troy.

'We could go like the wind, if he would carry us,' said Alexia stretching out a tentative hand to stroke the beautiful grey. The horse nuzzled her fingers with a velvety nose. Its eyes were an unsettling blue.

'But *will* it?' said Phelim. 'Maybe if I give it something to eat—make friends, you know?—while you get aboard.' So he put his hand into his shirt's breast-pocket.

His fingers closed over the stale hot cross bun the domovoy had thrown at him, and he took it out and offered it to the stallion on the flat of his palm. 'Nice horse. Good horse.' Alexia meanwhile laid one hand on the mane, and raised a foot to the stirrup.

At the sight of the bun, the horse reared up and staggered backwards on its hocks. Its back-to-front hooves lashed out at Phelim's hand. Alexia was knocked off her feet. Black lips drew back off long yellow teeth, and blue eyes rolled with fear and rage. Bucking stiff-legged, the stallion scattered stones and clods of earth, whinnying and shrieking fit to wake nightmares in a thousand stalls. Then it took off at full tilt, back the way it had come.

'I think we made a mistake,' said Alexia, sitting dazed on the ground without making any attempt to get up.

'Yes,' agreed Phelim. 'I think it would've preferred cake.'

A half mile down the road, a strange black animal leapt aside to let the galloping grey pass. Watching it go, it trotted on sedately, presenting itself to Phelim, saying from somewhere within itself: 'Youz whistled and I cummen.'

Phelim gave a laugh of disbelief. The creature looked more

like a round café table than a horse, with a black cloth thrown over it and only two legs protruding. It whirled and twirled, nodding so hard that its legs staggered. And yet it had no head. Phelim was convinced that somewhere under the black conical spire sticking up out of its centre and topped with black ribbons was a man's head. It was nothing short of a bizarre pantomime horse. Besides, he could not see anywhere for a rider to sit.

Once again Phelim held out the hot cross bun. The hobby-horse moved forward and peered at it with interest. 'Very nice, young zur,' it said, without making any attempt to eat. ''Gainst illness 'tiz a sterling remedy grated wi' 'ot milk. Saw yon ushtey take flight. You did well. Ushtey wouldn't care to zee an 'oly thing—being devilish.'

Phelim decided to follow his sister's advice. *'Manners, Phee,'* she always said, *'remember your manners.'* He extended his hand tentatively towards the circular horse which was humming tunefully and dancing to its own music. But seeing Alexia still sitting on the ground, it suddenly made a dash at her, flinging up its skirt and engulfing her in the valance of black horse-skin. There was something about it so odd and improper that Phelim felt doubly embarrassed and put hands up to either side of his head: Blinkers, he thought uncomfortably.

The horse had no sooner covered Alexia than it let her go, twirled round and galloped back to Phelim, gallopy, gallopy on its two spindly legs. Round and round him it danced. The capering made him want to laugh. 'I wonder, would you be happy for me to ride you or . . . or would you rather not? You see, I have to get to the sea. So I'm told.'

Immediately it plunged to its knees, its skirts fluttering as the circular body settled to the ground. It looked now like a horse which had been run over by a steam traction engine. Gingerly Phelim sat down on the black disc, his legs to either

60

side of the conical centre, the ribbons floating out over his shoulder. At once the Obby Oss jumped to its feet and went on capering, unslowed by the extra weight, making no allowance for Phelim's safety or dizziness. 'Which way?' asked the beast. 'Whither?'

From a great way off, watching through telescopes made from thick, ancient, coloured glass, the coranieids said nothing: though they collected words in such copious millions, they had no mouths to speak them. No dismay registered on their small, expressionless faces. The water-horse, the ushtey they had sent, had failed to capture its prey. But there would be other opportunities. All along the horizon their black nets trawled the sky like baleen whales sifting krill from the oceans. In among the rattle of tea cups, the organ music, the singing of choirboys, the clop of hooves they found, like cake crumbs, the words *'the sea . . . Stoor Head . . . Jack o' Green . . . speak soft'*, and again and again: *'Do let's hurry!'*

7

The Fear

They took it in turns to ride the Obby Oss, and their progress was not much quicker: the animal wasted its energy in wheeling and ducking, prancing and rearing up. But Alexia said it was not having transport which counted, but having the Horse to complete their band: Green Jack, Fool, Maiden, Horse. The Oss was both exhausting to ride and exhilarating, too, for some of its energy seeped upwards to infect its rider.

'What would have happened if I had chosen the ushtey?' Phelim asked.

'Mischief and mayhem,' said the Oss. 'Carried you away 'ee would've, to z'own element. Beast of water, 'tiz. Sea and river be lair and stable to the ushteys. Ducked you in the drink, it would've,' snickered the Obby Oss, hilarious as ever, and galloped towards a pond, stopping short so abruptly that Phelim only just clung on to the conical hump.

'But *why*?' said Phelim. It was a heartfelt question, a what-have-I-ever-done-to-him kind of question. Alexia seemed to accept this onslaught of monsters through which they must battle their way or die. But Phelim wanted reasons, explanations. In the last two days they had already glimpsed a Boa sucking cows dry like oranges before biting them in half. They had seen the Glaistig, dancing and whistling, beckoning from a ledge of rock, swaying and crooning while milky dreams dribbled from her teats. They had seen a field of sheep slaughtered so that the Redcaps could re-dye their hats blood-scarlet. They had passed a church where the locals had barricaded themselves indoors. But already a plague of Portunes, noisy as death-watch beetles, were up in the church belfry, roasting frogs and dropping the bones down on the people below, like pins. Why were these Hatchlings born with so much hatred in them?

'Could be bought off, they could,' said the Oss in his soft Cornish burr. 'Folks could hold they off with bribes: a child, spilled blood, a drowning . . . But folks have forgot. Forgot the price. Forgot how to pay it. Me, I'm hopping happy!' it declared, twirling round, whisking its tail. 'Me, I scared off the Frenchies and I put babes into barren women, and I get paid. All's well, all's well, all's well. In my part of the world, I'z honoured still. Every year I'z paid with my day of delights. Dance and drum, drum and dance every May Day unfailing. No missing. No one forgets me!'

'They shouldn't pay! The others, I mean. Not with blood and children and suchlike! It's vile! It's blackmail!' retorted Phelim hotly. 'It's giving in to blackmail. Like sending twelve men and maidens to feed the Minotaur. Theseus didn't. Theseus refused. Theseus went and fought the Minotaur and killed it sooner than go on paying the tribute!'

They looked at him, both of them, wondering if he was talking about someone they knew. 'Theseus who?' said Alexia.

'It was in my dad's book,' said Phelim defensively. 'He had lots of books.'

They continued to look at him expectantly, as if he might by magic somehow produce this father, this slayer of minotaurs. He did not meet their eyes. His head dropped. 'Dad left.'

'To fight monsters?' asked Alexia.

'He just left.'

The year seemed to be ageing around them. Though it was the height of summer, the trees on the skyline were starting to turn, their leaves to redden. Perhaps the whole landscape was becoming bloodstained. That same icy wind with a woman's voice often blew, lifting their collars, fanning out the horse's tail. Oss called it the Fata Padourii: a shape-changer, a Hatchling, naturally. There were acorns and conkers under the horse's hooves, then dry fallen leaves crunching. It was easier to see, when they peered up into the branches, that Sweeney was not there waiting.

'I hope he's all right,' said Alexia. 'Poor old Sweeney.'

'I didn't like him,' said Phelim rashly. 'I don't like mad people. They're scary.' He knew it was not a Nice thing to say, but the time for Nice seemed to have come and gone. He had been hoping they could get by without Sweeney and his deep-sunken, staring eyes, his trembling hands and hair, the way he chewed his lips until they bled. In any case there was something disgusting about a man who rent birds apart at the seams for the apparent fun of it.

Alexia looked such reproof at him that his cheeks burned. 'He was not always mad, you know.'

'Fought the Frenchies, like me!' the Oss chipped in.

'He fought at Waterloo.'

'Oh, poppycock!' snorted Phelim. 'Waterloo was a hundred years back. More.'

'Fact remains,' said the Oss cheerily, and threw Phelim on the ground.

'His detachment was cut off from the main force of men but they were in a hollow dip,' Alexia began. 'If they'd lain down, they could've stayed hidden. Officer commanding was a fool, of course, but rank is rank. He told them to stand tall like proud Englishmen. So up they stood, and now their heads came visible to the French artillery. Men began to drop every time the French fired. Men to the right of Sweeney, men to the left. Every bang of the cannon, he thought it was his turn. "Form line!" said the officer, not knowing any better. Forming square was their only chance. Only a square can hold against cavalry: Sweeney knew that much, even then. The Frenchies came on like reapers. Time for one musket shot, then the musket's empty and it's man against horse.

'A Frenchie fixed on Sweeney. On he came, and Sweeney took aim for his one-and-only shot. His best friend fell dead up against him, just as he fired, so Sweeney's shot went wide. The cavalry came through. Each horse took out one man from the line. One on the way through, then one coming back. To and fro they rode, like they were trampling down wheat.

'The officer rode for his life, abandoned his men. The smoke drifting down from the cannon made a grey blank fog, and the riders came out of the fog, in front, behind, on both sides. Four times the man right beside Sweeney went down saying, "Sweeney! Sweeney help me!"

' "Sweeney, don't let them . . . "

' "Sweeney tell my mother . . . "

' "We're all going to die, Sweeney!"

'And it was true. A young drummer took off his shirt and waved it for a flag—to surrender, see? But the Frenchies weren't interested. No prisoners, their orders said. The drummer boy ran towards them waving his shirt, "I surrender! I surrender!", and a sabre took him in the face. Sweeney tried to run but there was a hussar coming from behind. He ducked down—right under the horse, so he could smell the sweet, animal smell, see the pieces of cloth snagged in the horseshoes and the hussar's sword stabbing for him. The flat of the sword hit Sweeney over and over, though never the edge.

'Finally Sweeney tipped over and lay still, pretending to be dead. Lay there, cheek by jowl with a dead friend, and he kept corpse-still—even when the flies came buzzing—even later. The camp followers came through looking for bits to steal— wedding rings and money belts. One Frenchie took a fancy to Sweeney's boots and dragged them off, but still he didn't move. One was plucking the buttons off his jacket—felt for a purse. Felt no purse, but he felt Sweeney's heart beating—thump, thump—and he says, "This one's feigning" and pulled out a pistol and laid the barrel to Sweeney's cheek, so that he could feel it cold against his cheekbone, and hear the trigger creak and the hammer lift and the burn of the powder lighting . . . But the gun misfired, and the noise brought in an English officer who cut down the camp follower.

'After, this officer saw Sweeney all curled up in a ball and begging not to die, and he said "Conduct unbecoming a British soldier." "Bad example to his fellow men," they said. "Hang him for cowardice." And they dragged Sweeney to a tree and they put a noose around his neck and they slung the rope over a branch, and four or five of his comrades were at the rope's end, and Sweeney was saying, "You don't understand. You don't understand."

'Then the fear came upon him like the Holy Spirit at Whitsun, and he bent his legs and he jumped—jumped clear out of his wits and into the tree branches. When they had him surrounded, he had to jump to the next tree and the next, gibbering like an ape, so they thought he was laughing at them, and they threw stones, and loaded their muskets. So Sweeney jumped clear out of France to the loneliest place he could ever remember. And when he came to look inside his head, he found the first part of his Knowledge: that War is madness. But his fear was past healing, of course. I suppose we'll all feel fear like that before we're done.'

All the while Alexia spoke, the Oss had danced and twirled, but now he settled to the ground like a tent with its guy-ropes cut, and Phelim was able to step astride him and resume his seat. He did not speak. He did not attempt an apology. He simply vowed to find Sweeney before they reached the sea and make things right with him.

Sweeney would understand about the shirt. Sweeney would know why Phelim had kept silent about the shirt. With his great fear-fuelled Knowledge, he might even know how the Washer-at-the-Ford could be kept at bay.

In his new eagerness to see Sweeney, he scoured the evergreen trees which overhung the road ahead, and when he saw the branches heave and stir, was filled with gratitude and relief. Sweeney had indeed known where to find them! Sweeney had kept rendezvous with them! Sweeney would keep them company now, wherever their journey led.

Beneath him, the Oss became suddenly hesitant and slow. So sliding off its back, Phelim ran ahead to greet Sweeney— heard the horse whinny after him, call his name. His conscience was bad after thinking so unkindly of the old man, but he would make it up to him. 'Sweeney! Sweeney? We're here! Look, I have my Horse! How much further to the sea?' The tree, being evergreen, still had a dense, dark canopy of leaves; Phelim put one foot into a knothole in the trunk.

Not until then did he see the Boa hanging by its tail. Its inverted head swung up against his. Newly ingested cow's milk ran down out of its gullet and splashed on to the ground below.

It was not a snake—not a boa-constrictor—but a slithering limbless dragon of a beast, armoured with scales and as big-bodied as an ox. Its bulk tapered away to a prehensile tail with which it hung from the highest branch to await its prey. Fear bubbled up inside Phelim like a kettle coming to the boil. He could smell decomposing cow as the Boa opened its mouth and dislocated its jaws in order to seize on him . . .

'Drop down, boy!' The Oss, mastering its fear, had dashed in underneath Phelim, to catch him. He fell awkwardly, clung on by teeth and fingers and toes, slid off again within fifty paces of the tree. All three turned to run, but the path behind them was now carpeted with gross toads, huge and tailed toads with rudimentary wings and lengths of fishing line snarled around the hinges of their prodigious legs. Leaping forwards, the toads struck the children like over-ripe avocados, black and green and soft.

Phelim would have given six florins just then, to see Sweeney leaping from tree to tree, coming to their aid. They bolted between the trees, towards a brightness beyond the edge of the wood. Behind them the bracken convulsed as the Boa came shouldering through it, before wheezing to a halt and giving up the chase. Flies off the bracken swarmed round their heads—biting flies and tics. The coarse stems tripped them, made fine scratches across their shins and thighs. Even outside the woods, they dared not look back, for fear one of the water-leapers struck them in the face. One clung to Alexia's hair for a while: Phelim knocked it off with a stick.

'They seem to know!' she groaned aloud. 'They seem to know he is on his way to kill their mother! Do they know, Oss? Do you think they know?'

The Obby Oss spun round like a whirligig and kicked a fir cone back into the wood as if it were a curse or a jeer. 'They'z set the coranieids to watching uz, and maybe they sense his goodness a-cummin. Maybe they do. Sweeney would know. I do crave after Sweeney's Knowledge some dayz.'

It sank down, for Phelim to mount it again, but fleered away again, sensing the boy's irritation.

Phelim ran on ahead, trying to get beyond earshot of their conversation, trying to outrun his thoughts. Must they talk about him like that? As if he were the Masked Rider or Merlin the Magician? He did not think he could bear one more mention of his *goodness* or his *magic* or his *'coming'*.

He could not outrun the Oss, of course. It came bouncing along abreast with him, jolly as a spinning top, ribbons flying, and began telling him a joke. 'When the wolf went in among the sheep, wearing a stolen fleece, what did . . . '

Phelim rounded on him, furious. 'Don't you understand? Sweeney's not going to meet up with us. Sweeney's probably been eaten by a boa or a nuckelavee—or had his neck broke by the noonday twister! He's probably *dead*! Like we will be soon. Like we all will be.'

The Oss sank slowly downwards, like a circus tent collapsing. It was unaccustomed to unhappiness, to unpleasantness. When Alexia caught up, she told Phelim off roundly for upsetting the beast, and coaxed it to its feet again.

'In the unlikely event that Sweeney's dead, we'll just have to press on to Storridge without him. And the Worm . . . There's always Uncle Murdo. He may not have Sweeney's Knowledge, but he's wise and kind and good, and I love him dearly,' she declared resolutely, wearing her head stiffly high, twitching her mouth into an expression which forbade further argument.

8

Devil Take the Hindmost

As soon as they reached the town of Storridge, Phelim and Alexia went in search of food. They had got together some money by feeding another well, this time with elderberries, and had raised the price of two bicycles on which to complete their journey, as well as the price of a meal. At the thought of food and owning a bicycle, Phelim had laid aside his bad temper. Perhaps that was why Alexia had suggested feeding the well.

They found a high street cafeteria where the waitresses all wore black dresses and white aprons and there were proper lacy white tablecloths and pink napkins in china napkin rings and a smell of muffins. The lady supervisor regarded their shabbiness with undisguised hostility. Only when they jingled their two florins was she obliged to smile a lemony smile and allow them through the door. They decided they had been right not to bring the Obby Oss into Storridge: it was not a town steeped in the Old Ways.

They sat down in the window bay, where they had a good view of the street and a leafy park beyond. They were famished. They ordered soda scones and sandwiches, Victoria sponge cake and cling peaches, choux pastries and flapjacks, Bakewell tart and trifle with extra cream. The waitress who served them looked at their hands, black with grubbing for acorns, purple with elderberry juice, red with brick dust and rust, green with grass stains. Her eyes drifted to a notice on the wall which read:

ALL THE FOOD ON THESE PREMISES
IS PREPARED WITH THE UTMOST REGARD TO HYGIENE.

The manageress, in a black dress which still reached almost

70

to the floor came sweeping across and redirected them to a corner table at the back of the shop, near the kitchen. The other tables, she informed them, were 'resarved'. Alexia gave a hiccuping snort. Phelim caught sight of himself in the rose-tinted, bevelled wall-mirrors, his face crumpling as he tried in vain to suppress the giggles. He knew that his sister would have disowned him, grubby lout that he was. Automatically he looked to see if Alexia had fared any better . . . but of course the boy in the rose-tinted mirror sat alone at his table, an unaccompanied reflection.

All through the meal Phelim found himself looking for Alexia's shadow on the damask tablecloth, for a warped reflection in the nickel-silver teapot. She saw him looking.

'Shall I tell you how it was?' she said, eating a sugar lump out of the bowl. Phelim helped himself to three, rattling them behind his teeth. 'My parents sent me to study in Germany. A kind of apprenticeship. A grounding in the Black Arts.'

Phelim was riveted. *'During the War?'*

'Irish. My family's Irish. Ireland wasn't in the War first off . . . I didn't want to go, even so. But Pa's a gambler: he sent my brother into the priesthood, and I was the each-way bet, you see? I was the insurance policy. He wanted every kind of good luck he could lay his hands on. It wasn't my choosing, you know? I didn't want to go.'

Phelim nodded encouragement. 'Go on!' If he had had the chance to learn magic, he would not have needed much persuading.

'My parents weren't the kind you argue with, and once I got there . . . The Master who taught us was very . . . agreeable. Well, naturally he was. He could make himself seem anything, couldn't he? He was plausible. Kind. Clever. Good-looking.' Her face softened. 'We students all thought he was . . . ' She tailed off, remembering.

'Did you learn any? Magic, I mean?'

'Enough to get me burned as a witch in the old days. Enough to see beyond the surface sometimes.' (He thought back to the Drac in the river, and stopped grinning.) 'I didn't finish my course, or I'd know more. Anyway, while I was there, the Master came to the end of his own apprenticeship, and his fees came due.

'It was a sunny day. You don't imagine these things happening on a sunny day. Midnight, thunder, firelight, that sort of thing. But this was a sunny day. Then suddenly there came this space—this kind of *hole* in the daylight. A piece of dark. No horns, no tail, nothing like that. More like having a hawkmoth in the room, interfering with the light. We were all sitting at our desks in the hall where we had our lectures—and there was the Master, and there was this . . . no-light beside him. I'd never seen him scared before. But he was scared now. The Devil had come for his fees: he wanted a soul from his apprentice. The words sort of blurted out of him—like he was being sick. *"Devil, take the hindmost!"* he said.'

Alexia stopped. She was seeing again the stampede for the door, the tripping and elbowing, the banging of hips against the old wood-and-iron desks, the barging through the doorway while she, slow to grasp what the words meant, sat wondering what was happening. *Devil take the hindmost.* It took her maybe two seconds to realize. She was last to her feet, last through the door.

'I was the hindmost, you see,' said Alexia, cradling her teacup in both hands, the steam curling past her green eyes. 'He'd told the Devil to take the last one to leave the room. The sun was blasting in at the door. It was a heatwave, I remember. His hands on me were like ice. I called out to the Master to help, but he turned his back. He was cleaning the blackboard with a rag.

'So I pointed at my shadow on the wall and said, *"She's* last.

She's last, not me!" It was so black against the doorpost that for a second I really did think it was someone else. Then I kept saying it over and over and pointing. "Take her! She's the last! She's the hindmost!" '

In the restaurant the supervisor flicked her white lace handkerchief in irritation. The children in the corner were growing noisy. Others of her respectable clientele were being disturbed.

'And my shadow seemed to be pointing at me, just the same. "Take her. Take *her*!" '

Alexia's index finger straightened and her tea slopped but she did not notice. She was reliving the loss of her shadow, the excision, that moment in the doorway when, like Siamese twins with only one heart, they had been torn apart by the Devil. She had seen the Devil devour her shadow like a sheet of blackened toast, had seen the rage in his eyes as he tasted the bitterness of having been tricked.

The waitress asked if they would like anything else, but neither answered or even noticed her standing there, notebook and pencil poised, adding up the bill.

'It's an old story,' said Alexia as they walked down the street past the church. 'You'll hear it all over. Old Nick can't distinguish, you see. Between a shadow and the thing that casts it. It's the way his eyes work. He looks at a person and all he sees is the blackness in them. It can't look much different from a shadow.'

Shapeless organ music rambled out of an open church door. Inside, a choir of little boys in white surplices were practising.

'What did your parents say? I mean, how did they feel about having sent you to—'

'I didn't go home. I can't ever go home. They'd send me back to Germany, and I don't want to go. I haven't been back since. So, naturally, I didn't finish my studies. Otherwise I'd know better what to do to help you.'

Phelim had the feeling that Alexia did not tell her story to any and everyone, that it was a source of lasting shame and pain she would sooner forget. She had told him Sweeney's secrets, too. He ought to repay her with some confession of his own . . . Then the memory of the Washer-at-the-Ford came back to him like a door slamming on his fingers, and he began to shudder convulsively, so that Alexia saw it and thought her history had revolted and disgusted him. They walked further and further apart, passing to different sides of the new war memorial being erected at the foot of the town.

When he reached the bicycle shop, the closed sign was up, but Phelim pushed at the door and it opened. A storm of flies came swirling out into the brightness, brushing against his face—more as if he had opened a stable door.

The shop's stock of bicycles had been systematically destroyed. Wheels, wrenched off and buckled, lay among an intestinal knot of tyres, pink inner tubes erupting in hernias through every rubber casing. Pedals and chains wrenched off their frames lay alongside a dozen imploded metal cans, half-submerged in the pool of 3-in-1 easing oil. Every leather saddle had been slashed until the springs inside pushed worm-like out through the upholstery, and every pump had been broken down into its nine component parts. On the walls were bright monochrome posters of jolly young people cycling through an English countryside. But into every paper face and heart and thigh and stockinged ankle, wheel spokes had been driven, as if by the force of an explosion. Someone did not want him to reach the Worm.

'No joy,' he said, shutting the door smartly behind him, so that Alexia would not see inside.

'It isn't much further, anyway,' she said with a shrug.

His heart gave an unaccountable lurch. 'To the Worm?'

'Oh, we reached *that* yesterday. I told you: it's not like you imagine. But it's not much further to Uncle Murdo's house, I meant. We can spend the night there. You need a good supper, if you're going to be ready to fight the Worm.'

'What if he's moved away?' called Phelim, struggling to keep up. Alexia was riding the Oss, whose hooves picked a nimble path over the wet rocks slimy with weed.

Alexia called back over her shoulder, as confident as ever. 'Fishermen don't move. They get to know their piece of water. They know where the fish are. They don't move away to a strange bit of sea. Besides, it's the closest place to the Faeries on Hy Brasil: Uncle Murdo has always been interested in Faeries. Ever since he caught a glimpse of Hy Brasil when he was . . . '

'FAIRIES!?' Phelim gave a hoot of laughter. 'Did you say ''*fairies*''?'

'Faeries, yes. The Undecided. The Hidden People, the Children of Eve.'

'Fairies!' Phelim gave another great yelp of laughter. 'The *fairies*! You never believe in *fairies*! No one believes in *fairies* any more. Fairies!' he said the word contemptuously and often.

'Your grandparents did, and their great-grandparents before them.'

'Yes, but that was years ago,' sneered Phelim. 'They didn't know any better. Time moves on.'

The Oss came to a sudden halt. 'It do? So why do Monday come round to Monday, and May to May and zummer to zummer and dawn to dawn? Generation to generation? Janner, lad! How do a man look at the great wheel of Time and zee a straight line?'

Phelim was sorry he had not kept his amusement to himself. What was so ludicrous about fairies, in a world where nuckelavees prowled about and boas swung in the trees?

Nothing. Nothing at all. The ridiculous part was in Alexia and the Oss thinking *he* was the stuff of fairy stories, when he knew he was not. 'I'm a boy, not a man,' he said sulkily. 'And I'm not Jacko Green. I'm Phelim Green, and I'm not going to fight any Worm. Not tomorrow and not any other day.'

'You say it and yet you stay with us. You don't go,' said Alexia. 'If you won't, you won't; there's nothing we can do. But you will. I know you will. Everything depends on you.'

The tide was out, but Phelim picked his way right down to the water's edge. The slopping, choppy, murky sea soothed him. He stooped down and washed the dust out of his eyes, his hair, his ears. It would be good to eat a hot supper and sleep in a proper bed.

They saw no signs of monsters as they approached the hamlet where Alexia's Uncle Murdo and Aunt Audrey lived. Little livestock grazed the bleak, salt-caked cliff tops where all the stunted little trees leaned inland, sculpted by wind. There was still no sign of Sweeney.

They saw the hulk of a rotten rowing boat upturned on the shingle, but that might have been there years. They found mermaids' purses strewn along the rocks, but dogfish shed them every year. A terrible, plaintive, bellow roared at them out of the sea, but they came in sight of a lighthouse and knew it was only the foghorn sounding.

The boats on the beach became more numerous, interspersed with bundles of rope and crab pots, duckboards and winches. Then a cluster of fishermen's cottages came into sight. Along a little jetty, three figures in Guernsey pullovers sat looking out to sea, perched on the wooden posts where they tethered their boats. There was an open whaler, a half-cabined crabber, a clinkered dinghy. Phelim was full of relief at seeing such an everyday, ordinary sight. But what would these pleasant, God-fearing old men think if they were to look up and see a cloth horse trotting along the beach towards them?

The Oss had come to a halt anyway. It stood stock still, though the blustery wind rattled its valanced hide so that it appeared to tremble. 'Take care,' it said.

Phelim slid off its back. He felt distinctly bandy, and his thighs ached too much to run to the jetty as fast as Alexia did. He saw her duck her head and speak to first one man, then another, recoiling, then wrapping herself in her own arms.

By this time Phelim had reached the jetty himself. None of the old men paid him any attention either. 'Excuse me! Murdo the Fisherman. Is one of you—? Do you know him at all?'

But none of the fishermen seated on the capstans so much as looked up. 'Murdo,' he repeated. 'Murdo Jones?' Or were they dozing? Phelim's sister had impressed on him that people who are asleep do not care to be disturbed. Bending to look into the face of the nearest man, he saw that the eyes were open— 'Excuse me, sir . . . ' The eyes did not so much as flicker.

He touched the man's shoulder; he did not keel over, limp and dead, but neither did he register Phelim's presence. His eyes were fixed on the sea, his hands spread on his knees, elbows wide. He looked as though he were about to stand up and at the same time looked as though he would sit there for ever.

Phelim ran to the other men, but each seemed to be sunk in the same reverie. The wind driving into their faces had chapped the damp end of each nose, cracked the unmoving lips. A cream woollen hat stuck out of an oilskin pocket; Phelim pulled it out and tried clumsily to tug it over the ice-cold dome of the fisherman's bald head. 'Wake up! Wake up!' he told them with increasing temerity, until he was bawling it into their faces. *'Wake up!'*

Still the Oss hung well back, sensing evil. Down under the jetty, Alexia was starting to cry. 'What's the matter with them?' Phelim asked, angry with frustration.

He followed her to the row of terraced fishermen's cottages; she could not remember which was the one she had stayed in years before. They peered in at the windows, opened gates, calling. Some of the houses were derelict, empty, their gardens overrun with sea beet and thrift. In others, boots lay muddy by the doorstep, washing hung out in the fine drizzle. Indoors, meals lay half-eaten on the table, a tobacco tin open, a sea-boot stocking half darned. Phelim picked up mail from a doormat; the postman had come and gone without noticing anything amiss. He read the name on the envelopes. 'This is the place. ''Mr M. Jones'', see?'

'Well, of course it is,' snapped Alexia irrationally. 'I knew that! See? There he is!'

Murdo Jones was indeed sitting in his rocking chair. His pipe was between his lips, but had long since gone out. His cup of tea stood balanced on the corner of the fireplace, stone cold. With the Oss in the little room, there was scarcely space to move; the three of them filled it from wall to wall, their elbows knocking photographs and ashtrays. 'Is he dead?' Phelim kept asking.

They squeezed through into the kitchen, where Murdo's wife stood at the sink. The tap was running, and her hands were sunk in a bowlful of socks and woollen underwear as she gazed out across the back yard. Alexia turned off the tap and lifted the icy blue hands out of the cold water, resting them on the edge of the sink. Murdo's wife did not resist, but neither did she notice. Her eyes—sore from want of blinking—were fixed on the middle distance, seeing nothing, acknowledging nothing. She did not even object as the Oss clattered its dirty hooves across her immaculate flag floor.

They squeezed out of doors into the back garden. The Oss was stamping with the unease of a horse in a thunderstorm. When a slate fell from the roof and smashed just behind its hocks, it leapt with fright and cannoned into Phelim who struggled to maintain his footing on the wet paving stones. Their nerves were strung out to breaking point.

Looking up to see what had dislodged the tile, Alexia saw a foot protruding from behind the chimney stack. She picked up a stone and threw it—a wild, angry, inaccurate throw—'What have you done to them?' The chimney's pointing crumbled. A high, wavering voice, masked at first by the cry of seagulls, sang:

'What did they do with the sailor's soul, then?
Took it to the beach when the sea was rolling,
Took it to the bottom where the fish are shoaling
Erl-eye in the morning!'

It was Sweeney, his eye-sockets ringed with shadows, his lips flapping, as he breathed air in and out, in and out, faster than his throat could contain. He slid down the roof, coming to rest with the heels of his bare feet in the gutter. Throwing an arm over his head, he dragged it down till his chin was driven into his chest.

'What shall we do with the bold deserter?
Leave her on the field with a bayonet through her,
Shoot her with a pistol, let the black crows chew her . . . Didn't do nothing. No help to anyone, that Sweeney. Coward to the end, that Sweeney. The merrows came out of the sea and he didn't do a thing. Nothing, nothing, nothing.' And he beat on the gutter till it slopped old rainwater down into the yard. At the mention of merrows, the Oss bridled and turned about and about, rattling its hooves on the paving stones.

They tried to persuade him to come down, but Sweeney was too full of self-loathing, and only huddled like a rain-swept owl, near the chimney stack.

So there sat Murdo and there stood his wife. Their milky old eyes were shineless pebbles, and their hands knobbly roots which had withered and died. Not that Murdo himself was dead, but the merrows had come out of the sea and stolen away his soul, to keep him from aiding the enemies of the Worm.

Phelim stood picking at the seam of his shirt cuff, undoing one stitch at a time. But Alexia said, in her brisk, practical voice, 'Well, then. If the merrows have Uncle Murdo's soul, we must go and get it back.'

9

The Merrow's Catch

The merrows live off shore—far enough to enjoy ten fathoms of water over their heads but close enough in to come ashore and sit on the rocks, fishing. If it were not for their *collecting*, they might be thought of pleasantly—the leprechauns of the sea.

The Oss stood on the jetty's end, looking out to sea. 'Fishermen bin friends wi'em afore now, and merrows've shown kindness to sailors. Yet they be a sort of demon, rightly speaking, for they covet the immortal zoul of a man, to keep as men keep rabbits in a hutch. A zoo of zouls. That be their entertainment.'

Phelim and Alexia came and stood alongside him. A rowing boat which had drifted under the jetty at low water was banging now under their feet as the tide rose.

'Must be a drowned town hereabouz,' said the Oss, still bridling uneasily, dashing between the jetty and the house where Sweeney sat on the roof. 'Be there? Be there, Sweeney? A drowned big-house? A farm? Do you have the Knowledge?'

'There's a place yonder where the sea rose up and swallowed church and hall and oaks alike.' Sweeney's shout was like the squawk of a parrot.

'That's where, then,' said the Oss. 'That's where the merrows will be.'

They coaxed the rowing boat out from under the jetty and Phelim and Alexia got clumsily aboard. It was not big enough for the Oss.

'You can't let 'em go alone!' called Sweeney from the roof.

'Cummen down, then, and be an help to 'em!'

'We can do it alone,' said Alexia, though Phelim muttered, 'News to me.'

The sea looked cold, unready to render up its secrets. Alexia put the oars into the rowlocks and pulled on them. The boat promptly collided with the jetty, dislodging Alexia from her seat, and a pipe from one of the lifeless fishermen still seated on the bollards.

'She's sitting the wrong way to the oars!' wailed Sweeney, scrambling over the guttering and halfway down the drainpipe. 'Don't you know nothing? Must I show you? I see I must,' he complained. The Oss ran to fetch him, and Sweeney lowered himself, gingerly, gingerly on to the conical black body, tucking up his feet to keep them as far as possible off the ground. He kept up a doom-laden chuntering as well:

'Hearts of smoke are our ships,
Jolly scarred are our men.
We ain't never ready
Steady, boy, steady.'

Swooping down a long arm, he snatched up two empty beer bottles from beside the feet of the soul-less fishermen. Then, screwing up his eyes to blank out the fear, he dropped down into the rowing boat, turned it round with a single pull on one oar, and began rowing out to sea. Phelim and Alexia, obliged to share a single thwart, toyed with the idea of thanking him, saying how glad they were to see him. But since his eyes were still shut, they kept silent; Sweeney was probably pretending to be somewhere else, high up, away from the green heave of the unfriendly sea.

The Oss, too, prancing on the jetty's end, turned tail, so as not to see them go.

It was from out at sea that Phelim got his first glimpse of the Stoor Worm: Alexia pointed it out to him. A mass of land thrust out into the sea, interrupting the smooth curve of the coast. Within it and behind it, the land was far higher than round about, and it had a reddish tinge to it. There was no eye, no ear, no claw, no thorny tail. It was simply a piece of land. How can you be afraid of a piece of land? Phelim, who had been expecting the fright of his life, felt absolutely nothing. The Stoor Worm was simply a morsel of legend, untrue. 'It doesn't even look like a dragon,' he said, half laughing with relief.

'Well, that is only the snout,' she said.

Just beyond the promontory which formed one side of the bay, Sweeney shipped his oars. 'Somewhere hereabouts, I divine.'

'Why?' asked Alexia. 'How was it swamped? Did the villagers dance on a Sunday? Or murder someone? Or bury a sailor on dry land, or—'

'Reckon the sea level rose,' said Sweeney banally. 'Reckon the land sank or the sea rose, simple as that.' There were villages which had been drowned for their sin, others by an accident of geology.

Phelim was less concerned with why the village was there than how they were to find it. Perhaps in the transparent turquoise of the Indian Ocean, a sunken city would have shown plainly. But the Irish Sea was a particularly murky grey. How were they to see *what* lay beneath its surface? Sweeney had begun rinsing the bottles in the sea.

'What are they for?' asked Phelim. 'To send messages?'

'They's spyglasses!' And he held one over the side, his eye pressed to the opening, the base just below the surface.

Phelim copied him. The broken, choppy surface made the sea opaque, but with the bottle, he could see down a few metres. 'It's a kind of periscope in reverse!' he said. He and Alexia both peered into the bottles while Sweeney rowed, crossing and re-crossing the bay. Sea welled up into their faces from time to time; their hair got soaked. At first they commented on the fish they saw, then became increasingly silent and grass-green seasick as the little boat rolled over the swell.

'Listen, too,' said Sweeney, his head cocked on one side.

'What are we listening for?' asked Phelim.

'Bells,' said Alexia. She could hear them, the faint, muffled *dong dong dong* ringing in time with the swell, driven by the waves.

'It's a bell-buoy,' Phelim suggested, looking around for one.

'Nay, it's a church down below,' said Sweeney.

Phelim wiped the circle of brown ale from round his eye and peered once more through the waves with his bottle telescope. 'I see something!' he said. 'I see . . . I see . . . ' He hesitated to say it until he was sure. The rust-red cockerel turned about and about with each pull of the current, from north to south, back to north again. 'A weathervane!'

Sweeney began to unbutton his coat, humming to himself:

'All the little ducks said quack, quack, quack, quack
And the little ones chewed in the bones-O
Bones-O, bones-O!
All the little ducks said—'

'Sweeney, can you swim?' asked Alexia.

'quack, quack, quack,

Down with Davey Jones-O . . . If I must.' But his hands were shaking and his eyes were white-rimmed with terror.

'I wonder which of us can hold our breath the longest?' said Alexia cheerfully, nudging Phelim painfully hard in the ribs. 'We ought to find out. Shouldn't we, Green Man?'

So they all took a deep breath, and almost at once Sweeney began to cough. Although he was agile enough, he was accustomed to breathing fast and shallowly (as the terrified do). Sucking in a deep breath stirred up all the battlefield dust and cordite and barrack-room smoke and bronchitis of a hundred years.

Alexia and Phelim, on the other hand, looked one another in the eye and waited, cheeks puffed out. It was like a game. They both had good strong lungs. The boat drifted on the current. It was a good game.

Phelim forgot that the reward of winning was to swim down through fathoms of stone-cold, cloudy water and be met by shoals of merrows eager to cut out his soul. He held his breath till stars exploded at the edge of his vision and the sea looked bloodshot. He was determined not to let a girl beat him.

Alexia took a deep, gasping breath. 'You win!' she laughed. 'Oh.'

So it was for Phelim to pull off his clothes and scramble forwards, drop the boat's painter over into the sea. But instead of sinking, the rope floated. They had to weight the end with a belaying pin so that it would hang down straight beneath the boat. At first it banged about amongst chimneys and drowned treetops, but after a time it hung free, and Phelim lowered himself over the side of the boat, gasping at the cold. He tried to expand his lungs to the size of zeppelins. The rope guided him down.

He found that the weathervane belonged to the church, and that he touched bottom in what had once been a churchyard overlooking the sea. The headstones lay broken and askew, barnacle-covered and cloaked in weed, the carvings no longer legible. In every direction, dilapidated houses, their roofs off, their walls crumbling, opened and closed their doors in the current, as if inviting him in. He swam up for air, the cold prising at his ribs, compressing his lungs. 'What am I looking for?' he said, clasping the side of the boat.

'Lobster pots. Crab pots. Some such,' said Sweeney. 'Take your time, lad, and watch out for merrows.'

Another time, thought Phelim, this would have been a

thrill: to swim through a ghost town requisitioned by the sea, where fish had been billeted rather than people, where the winds were currents and the litter was shells. Now he wanted to find what he was looking for, and get out and away before the ghosts in the houses could draw him indoors, the merrows ambush him, the cold rob him of his wits.

Mawr had been a fishing village just like Murdo's; there were dozens of crabbing pots stacked between the houses, geometric patterns of their semi-circles. When he pulled the piles apart, crustaceans lurked there like slugs under flowerpots. But the pots themselves (as far as he could tell) were empty of souls.

Other pots lay tangled in garden hedges. When he picked one up, a purple lobster lunged at him, brandishing its claw like a prizefighter. In another a multitude of crabs were devouring each other, leg by leg.

He burst through the surface again knocking the beer bottle out of Alexia's hand. 'How am I supposed to know if there are souls inside?' he gasped, teeth chattering, voice sobbing with cold and frustration. 'What does a soul *look like*?'

'They glow green, so I've heard. Bright and shiny. And you can smell 'em by the sadness.'

Alexia snatched Phelim's wrist. 'Let me go. You're cold. Let me try.'

'No point us both getting wet,' he said, and dived back down, pulling himself down by the swinging pub sign, to be quicker on the seabed. He had no idea what Sweeney meant— how can you *smell* sadness, especially under water?—but he searched on, round a pig pen, a fish-gutting shed, a fenced garden, a stone breakwater.

Then he felt it. As a shark scents blood through ten miles of sea, he was suddenly crammed to the gills with it. A desperate desolate grief—there was no other word for it—so that his sinuses ached and his throat was clogged. He let himself float to the surface, and lay on his back, crying, rolling his head from side to side, overwhelmed by inconsolable, inexplicable grief. Fortunately he was fifty metres from the boat, so that the others could not see him plainly. They called out to him: 'Any luck? Any joy?'

No joy. There had been no joy in this place for a thousand tides. The sea grasses were poisoned, the crabs stayed clear. As he swam down again, the sea around him was illuminated by a sickly green haze.

A cluster of lobster pots had been wedged haphazardly into the branches of a drowned tree. Within each a green glow, like a firefly, pulsed faintly so that the tree was beautiful despite its leafless rotten limbs. Phelim allowed a stream of bubbles to filter from his open mouth.

Here they were: Murdo and his neighbours, keening and bemoaning their eternity pent up in little cages, watching the cold, dirty sea roll over a dead village. Here were the old men on the jetty, not up there, propped on bollards or beside cold cups of tea. If only his heart would stop aching and his brain start functioning, he might save them from their prison cells of willow and twine.

He found, to his huge relief, that by standing in the topmost branches of the tree, he could break surface and breathe. *'Here!'* he yelled towards the distant rowing boat. *'I've found them! Over here!'* He shouted so loud that Sweeney dropped an oar. He shouted so loud that the fish fled him in all directions. He shouted so loud that the merrows, bass-fishing on the far side of the promontary, heard him and drew in their nets.

Down Phelim went and picked at the knotted mouths of the lobster pots with fingers numb with cold. It was useless. He stayed till his lungs felt shrunk to the size of walnuts and his eyes were popping, but he still could not work out how to break into the cages. When he came up, he failed to see the keel of the boat and banged his head on it. *'Give me a knife. Give me a knife, Sweeney!'*

Sweeney drew out from under his rags a rusty Napoleonic bayonet, but Phelim missed the catch and had to swim down and retrieve it as it sank. Then he was jabbing and slicing at the knotted twine, trying to open the funnel mouths of the pots and let the captives out. He had thought to retrieve only Murdo's soul, but of course there was no distinguishing between these anonymous glimmers, these flying sparks of intellect trapped in withy baskets. And how could he leave *any* of them behind?

He feared the rusty blade might nick them, scar their immortal souls. But at last the pulses of green light flew past him—through him—like powdery snowballs, spiralling upwards towards the light, taking with them the saltwater stench of misery.

The happy idea of them tasting the air, taking their first breath—some after years under water—made him forget to hold his breath himself; water streamed up his nose and he dragged himself up through the branches of the tree. The tree was brittle as coral, and broke off in his hands. He began coughing with his mouth still under water and broke surface like a whale blowing.

He had been expecting mermen—creatures with tails: they were not like that at all. The merrows waiting for him on the surface, gurning and swearing, had legs and paddle-toed boots and clothes and long jawbones and flattened, gill-like noses and flapless ears. He recalled a picture in one of his father's books—gladiators fighting in the Colosseum. There had been men like that there—the *retiarii*—net in one hand, trident in the other. The merrows' hats were green, yes—copper helmets dull with verdigris.

Phelim, finding the bayonet still in his hand, held it out, offering a show of force. But they were all around him. He had to turn and turn on his precarious underwater perch, while the merrows drew closer from all sides, weighing their tridents in raised hands, flicking their nets tauntingly. They babbled at him in a bubbling, thick-lipped language.

The green haze of escaping souls clung for a moment to the rowing boat, like phosphorescence. The merrows hesitated, torn between going after their captives, and taking revenge on Phelim. Half broke away and swam to the rowing boat and began rocking it violently, trying to overturn it. The green lights rose like a cloud of butterflies and fluttered towards land. Alexia broke her bottle against the stern and jabbed it at the merrows' green spatulate fingers.

Sweeney pulled for the submerged tree: the current kept carrying him away from it. He ploughed straight into the circle of merrows, stood up and, bracing his feet wide apart against the boat's side, began to wield an oar for a quarterstaff. Three of their nets were over Phelim's face now, flattening his features, catching on his sticking-out ears. A trident jabbed him in the stomach: swimmer's cramp. And he thought, So it's now. I'm going to die now. The Washer-at-the-Ford meant now.

But Sweeney laid about the merrows in an insane, yodelling frenzy, inaccurate because his eyes were fast shut, but so demented that no one could move—not Phelim, not the merrows, not Alexia crouched down in the bottom of the boat.

'Die! Die! Die! Die! Die!' he screamed, and foam bubbled from his mouth. His feet came clear of the boards and the boat pitched up and down. He was back on the battlefields of Spain, killing Frenchmen before they could kill him.

Suddenly the merrows dived—they were sensitive to noise and uncertain whether all their pots had been spilled. Phelim seized the moment to scramble into the boat. A stroke from Sweeney's flying oar caught him a glancing blow on the back. Sweeney opened his eyes—'Oh God! I'm sorry, sir!'—then the madman was on his hands and knees in the bilges, and Phelim had retrieved the oars. The rudder caught on the topmost branches of the tree and, for a moment, stuck fast. Alexia bounded up and down like a dog, making the boat see-saw, breaking it free. Then Phelim was rowing for the shore with quick, splashy, ineffectual strokes which soaked the others to the skin with spray.

A kind of embarrassment settled over the boat; Alexia picking broken glass out of the bilges and dropping it overboard, Phelim studying his oar-blades, trying to make cleaner strokes. Sweeney was curled up in the bottom of the boat with his arms over his head and the umbrella spikes of his coat sticking up at wild angles making him look like a magnetic mine.

Phelim was not strong enough to stop the boat turning side-on to the breaking surf and over it went, spilling them into the white water, sinking them up to their wrists and ankles in rolling pebbles. They had to run back a long way to reach the row of houses where Murdo lived, and Sweeney, in his waterlogged greatcoat, could only spring like a wet frog from boulder to boulder in a series of damp splats. Long before they got there, the green cloud of lights had settled over the jetty, over the row of cottages. They could see the old men moving about, re-lighting their pipes, looking for their bottles of ale, their souls come home to them like pigeons to a roost.

'Will they remember?' asked Phelim, as he ran. 'Will they remember being down there?'

'I hope not,' said Alexia. 'And if they don't, we shouldn't remind them.'

He understood what she meant. If the fishermen had no memory of their captivity, all well and good. For who could bear even to think about a caged eternity spent stifling in the stone-cold sea, rolling like a pebble with every push and suck of the tide?

10

Three Wishes

When the children thumped on the door and burst into Murdo's cottage, his wife looked up from the sink, drying her hands in readiness to welcome visitors. Murdo took a sip of tea and pulled a face because it was cold. He appeared to have woken that very moment, though Phelim noticed that he had on a waterproof jacket now, whereas before he had not.

'Welcome. Welcome all!' he said struggling to his feet. 'Alexia? Can it be my little Lexie? *Duw*, but you've grown, girl! You brought some friends for me to meet, is it? Come in, come in! Get yourselves warm. Well, look at that. Fire's gone out: what was I thinking of!' His eyes kept moving to the grandfather clock in the corner. 'I have to catch the tide, you know, but your Aunty Audrey will find you a bite. Don't stint yourselves . . . '

There were no dubious sidelong glances at Sweeney or the Oss, no cross-questioning of his niece about the strange company she was keeping. Uncle Murdo was so overflowing with hospitality and warmth, so tolerant that he took in his stride the presence in his home of a hulking horse and two dripping-wet ruffians. Phelim was very pleased to have robbed the merrows of such a prize.

'We need your help, Uncle,' said Alexia, getting straight to the point. 'This is Jack o' Green, and this is his Horse and this is his Fool. I'm being his Maiden. We've come here so that Jack can stop the Stoor Worm waking.'

The old man's eyes widened and turned on Phelim. He's going to laugh, thought Phelim. But Murdo did not laugh. He sat down again, drawing Phelim in front of him, holding him there, grasping the boy's shoulders. He seemed to study every freckle, every eyelash, every streak of grime and every salt-stain of Phelim's face.

'I did hear it was waking,' he said in a slow, sonorous voice like a chapel organ. 'So you're Jack o' Green, is it, son? You did right well to bring him here, Lexie, and I'm rare honoured to make his acquaintance. *Duw*, but he's a man I've been after meeting a great long while. May I ask you, sir: is it true what I hear? That you're a chime child?'

'Alexia says so,' said Phelim. 'I did hear the Gabriel Hounds.' The old man gripped his biceps so hard that Phelim's fists flew open reflexly, but the voice remained as gentle as ever.

'And may I ask you, sir, how it is that *you* feel about my niece's plans for you?'

Oh, what a relief! What a glorious, luxurious, unforeseen relief: to find someone who cared enough to ask. 'Scared, sir,' said Phelim. 'Very scared.' He was going to go on to explain about the mistake, about not being Jacko Green at all, about feeding his domovoy milk by mistake, about the Hatchlings lying in ambush for him, about the shirt, about the shirt, about the shirt . . . But then Sweeney, perched up on the Welsh dresser, knocked down a plate, and the Oss's hooves got tangled in Aunt Audrey's knitting, and Alexia began talking about the old days.

'Did you ever see Hy Brasil again, Uncle?' she asked, sitting down on the arm of the chair, throwing an arm around his neck.

The old man visibly flinched. 'Hy Brasil? No. Me? Why would I be after going to any magic isle?'

'But since you found the place once . . . ?' said the Obby Oss.

Phelim was suddenly full of curiosity. 'Why? What's Hy Brasil?'

'Home of the Faeries,' Sweeney answered from the dresser.

'Once in seven years it rises from the sea—out on the horizon—where the sea joins the sky. The Isle of Hy Brasil. And if you can reach it and throw fire on to it before it sinks again—then you can make a wish and the Faeries have to grant—' He interrupted himself, an idea straying into view. 'Now wouldn't *that* be a sweet stroke of fortune.'

Alexia was eager to hear again the old story she had heard as a child on every summer visit. 'Uncle Murdo saw it once— when he was out fishing. When he was young. Tell Jack o' Green, Uncle. Tell him about seeing the Island.'

But Murdo, though he had once repeated the story endlessly to visiting nieces and nephews, no longer seemed willing to talk about it. 'Must be fifty years back. I've forgotten.'

'Oh, please!' Phelim was intrigued.

The old man directed him a baleful smile. 'Well . . . I am putting down nets one night, isn't it? And up it rises on the port bow. Just like that. I don't speak of it, commonly. Folk get strange about wishes, Golcondas, the like.'

'What's a—?'

Alexia kicked Phelim sharply in the shin.

'But did you never go back another time, with fire to throw and a wish to wish?' asked Sweeney; his face was screwed up like a sheet of paper. 'Most men have something . . . Every man has something . . . Some men would give anything . . . '

'Me? What would I be wishing for?' said Murdo with a shrug. 'Man like me? Haven't I about as much as any man needs?'

Phelim, like Sweeney, knew exactly what he would wish for, if such an island reared up like a whale in front of him. Oh yes, Phelim knew. 'When will it rise up next?' he asked. 'Every seven years, you said.'

Uncle Murdo pulled out a large, crumpled handkerchief and wiped his nose energetically, so Phelim lost sight of his eyes. 'Bless you, son, how would I know? The years go round so fast when you reach my age: there's no keeping track. One's very like another. What year did I see it? Don't recall. How old was I? Can't say I remember. Couldn't even tell you the right spot in the ocean to look.' He took off his jacket and hung it back behind the door. 'Time for supper, I say!'

'I thought you had to catch the tide,' said Alexia, glad that he had changed his mind about going out.

'Not with such fine company as I have here!' said the old man, beaming with contentment. 'Not with the likes of Jack Green under my roof! The fishing will have to wait tonight, isn't it?' And Phelim felt a glow of pleasure such as he had rarely felt before, that he was so welcome, so valued. His admiration was boundless for this fine, grizzled old man who prized the simple pleasures of life more than the magic of a wishing isle.

Phelim dreamed an underwater world of merrows, dreamed holding his breath, dreamed being unable to hold it another moment and begin, still under water, panicking, thrashing for the surface. He woke to find Murdo's hand over his mouth, the old man's face close to his.

'Never fear, boy. There's nothing to fear.'

Phelim raised himself up on one elbow. Alexia was asleep on the horsehair cushions from the downstairs armchairs. The Oss was outside in a shed. Sweeney was roosting up on the roof, theoretically to keep a look-out for merrows, though his snores could be heard coming down the chimney.

'You don't care much for this trick of theirs, do you, son? I could tell straight off. It's plain enough to see. They're taking you to the Worm against your will. Am I right?'

His silvery beard and sun-wrinkled eyes gave such an impression of kindness that Phelim could not help admitting straight away, 'You're right.'

'Well, you trust to your instincts, lad. Instincts tell true. Come with me.' He led Phelim by the hand, down the stairs and out of the open front door, not speaking again until they were in among the foxgloves in the little front garden. 'That girl's a witch, you know.'

'Well, yes, I know, but—'

'And the black horse?'

Phelim shivered in the early morning mist. It was still dark. The beach was strewn with the litter of the fishing trade—old planks, oil drums, nettings, lengths of rope. It swarmed with crabs feeding on the decaying scraps, their bodies crackling. Phelim stumbled over them towards the brightness of the sea, hardly able to pick his way. Murdo had no such trouble; he was quick on his feet and knew exactly where he was heading.

They went skidding down the steep shingle of the beach towards Murdo's boat. 'The Obby Oss? What about him?'

'Hatchling, a'course. Do you think Mother Nature ever gave birth to such a freak? He's not black to no purpose. His purposes are all black, you take my word. A jolly sort, but wait till he has you alone; then you'll see his true colours.' He led Phelim on to the jetty.

'The Oss is a Hatchling?' Phelim repeated it parrot-fashion, his sleepy brain unable to comprehend it. Of course the Oss was strange, yes—every bit as strange as the monsters they had seen streaming eastward from the Worm's hatchery. 'But they want me to destroy the Worm!'

'Do they, hell!' Murdo rocked his great leonine head sadly, saddened by the wickedness at large in the world. 'There's no destroying the Stoor Worm. Haven't I lived in the lee of it all my born days? Do you think I don't know? Its hide's all glassy smooth and hard as granite. Where you going to stab it? Its heart? Its brain? How you going to get up there? It's hundreds of feet straight up, on rock smooth as a salmon's armpit.'

'I don't know,' Phelim admitted. 'Sweeney says I can do it. I keep trying to tell him—'

'Now isn't that what he would say? Eh? And why would he say that? Can you guess? Eh, boy? Why would children of the Worm take a thing home to their mother? Ask yourself. An enemy, at that. A champion. I know what I took my old mother on the days I went visiting.'

He paused to untie his dinghy from the jetty, and possibly also for dramatic effect. '*Titbits*, isn't it, Master Green. That's what I took my mother. Titbits. And that's what they're taking to theirs.' As he said it, he poked Phelim surprisingly hard in the stomach with one finger. 'They're never taking you to the Worm to kill it. They're taking you there to *feed* it, son.'

Phelim gave a croaking, open-mouthed cry.

'But me and Mrs Murdo, we're jiggered if they'll do it. Mrs Murdo says to me, "Get the boy safe away, Murdo. Get him away in the *May Louisa*!" And so help me, that's what I'm going to do!'

The old man was surprisingly nimble as he jumped down into the rowing boat, but Phelim dislodged an oar which banged loudly against the hull.

'But Alexia's your niece!' he protested, in a hissing whisper. 'She used to come here when she was little!' He could hear his voice swooping upwards in a childish little wail.

'That were before she went off to College to study the Black Arts! Sold her soul to Old Nick, isn't it? Her mother and father, they was down on their knees begging her not to go, but would she listen? I'm telling you the truth now: I disowned her then and I disown her now. She's a filthy Devil-worshipping, pin-sticking, curse-making witch, and further away you are from her, the safer you'll be, believe you me!'

Phelim crouched down in the boat, hugging his knees, his throat aching with unshed tears. 'Sweeney too?'

'What do *you* think?'

The rowing boat hissed through the slick, night sea, rearing up a little at every massive pull Murdo gave to the oars. Soon it banged against the stern of the *May Louisa*. Murdo told him to grab the ladder there and climb aboard. 'Will they come after us, do you think?' whispered Phelim.

'After what you done for me and the missus, boy, down there among the pots, I owe it to you to take the risk.'

So. Murdo had known all along, about the merrows and their lobster pots. A man who could keep so silent was a man who could be trusted with secrets. 'Mr Jones, sir, they made a mistake about me,' Phelim began. 'I'm not—'

'They truly did, son. You're nobody's fool, are you? Let go the rope, there's lovely. And be quick.' There was a new urgency in the old man's voice which made Phelim glance towards the shore. The fisherman's house was still unlit, but up on the roof, barely visible against the dark sky, Mad Sweeney was on his feet, waving his arms. Phelim heard his name being called.

His fingers were cold. He could not undo the half-hitches fastening the *May Louisa* to its mooring line. 'Hurry, boy!' Murdo called, hauling up the sail.

Sweeney called again. He had jumped to the next-door roof and from there to a tree in the garden. No trees on the beach, though. No trees at sea. Phelim was sure they were safe. His fingers pulled the knot apart, the rope spraying him with cold water. The boat swung round on the swell. A million stars reflected in the sea like shoals of silver krill.

But there were trees of a sort, of course. When Phelim looked back, he saw the bat-coated man clinging to the topmast tip of a sailing boat's mast. From there, he came through a thicket of masts—leaping from trawler to skiff to dinghy, clearing prodigious stretches of water to land like an albatross on the cross-trees of a dozen masts. He shouted as he came. *'Wait! Wait! Pay no heed to his wishes, Green Man! Don't spend your magic on gold! If you must wish . . . '*

Murdo fumbled in a locker down by his feet. He pulled out a Very pistol—some piece of army-surplus put to use as a distress flare—and pointed it directly at Sweeney.

'. . . *Wish the Worm dead!*' bawled Sweeney.

The noise of the pistol going off was so loud that Phelim's hands flew to his ears. The sodium carved a golden furrow through the darkness, striking sparks off the dense dark. Sweeney uttered a banshee wail of terror, his face as white as the sodium flare arcing towards him. He hugged the mast of the crabber to which he clung, and his trembling set all its top-hamper rattling. But the flare fell short, and fizzled into the sea, swimming away like a white fish, under the hull.

Seeing the shock on Phelim's face, the old man sighed and shook his head. 'There's no killing the Devil's own,' he said. 'More's the pity.'

In Phelim's head the pictures kept forming of Sweeney fighting the merrows, swinging his oar at them, eyes tight shut, giving those imprisoned souls time to escape. But he found himself saying, 'It's true! He is evil. He rips open little birds!'—blurting it out: his own piece of damning proof.

'Looking for his wits, I know it,' muttered the fisherman. 'Looking for the one with the "cure" inside.' When he saw that Phelim had not known this, he exaggerated the scorn in his voice. 'Some swallow. Somewhere there's a swallow, seemingly. And in its chest there's a ruby. Gives a madman back his wits. Pha! Give Mad Sweeney back his wits and what would you have? A milk-hearted coward on the ground, isn't it?'

Phelim looked back again, but the madman was nowhere in sight.

Ever since the business of the shirt, Phelim had known what it was like to be insanely afraid. To be rid of that fright, wouldn't *he* have killed a swallow? He thought he might. In fact, he thought he might even now empty the sky of swallows if it would free him of the terror gnawing away inside.

'What did he mean about wishing the Worm dead?'

Murdo leaned his face into a non-existent wind and peered at the horizon as if through thick fog. 'Donno,' he said.

'Well, where are we going? Where's safe? Do you know somewhere?'

'That I do, son. And I'll get you there . . . if you'll just do me a little favour in return.'

For some reason, Phelim turned away and went for a walk around the deck of the *May Louisa* rather than hear this favour Murdo wanted. It was, perforce, a short walk. He soon found himself back at the helm, asking, 'What did Sweeney mean about gold?'

Murdo smiled. 'Now there's a word that pleases, isn't it? "Gold?" '

Phelim thought back to the well and the pennies. He had to agree. It was. Then he thought of the reason they had chosen to ask Murdo's help in the first place: 'a man rich in the Old Magic'; a man who believed in fairies.

'Tell me this has nothing to do with the Fairies.' Phelim's laugh said he hoped his guess was wide of the mark. Murdo shot him a look of keenest suspicion.

'What they been telling you, those Hatchlings?'

Phelim blushed.

The sun was just about to rise. Its rim was pushing at the horizon like a bubble trapped beneath the surface film of water. Murdo studied the compass. He paid infinite attention to the pinprick of sun visible, to the compass bearing, to the wind direction, to the run of the sea. Not once did he look at Phelim.

'Tell him, Murdo,' said a voice. 'Tell him where you're taking him. Tell him why.'

And there, clinging to the masthead like a moth's cocoon

to a twig, hung Sweeney. He must have made one last, long leap, to reach the *May Louisa* and to hang in her top-rigging, listening, hidden by darkness.

Murdo seemed to hesitate—to sum up whether Sweeney represented a threat to his plans. Deciding that Sweeney would never dare to come down from his perch, he gradually recovered his nerve. Having waited nearly sixty years, he was not about to be robbed of his prize.

'Every time, I've been there when it rose up. And every time, I've thrown fire ashore. Every time. And it's eight times now. Eight times I've seen it breach like a damn great whale, and rise up! I've made my wish and they've yammered their answer—don't want to say, but they've got no choice, see? Got no choice but to say!' His knuckles were white on the helm, the veins bulging in the soft skin around his eyes. One brown-spotted hand shot out and snatched an ancient exercise book off the shelf in front of him. He swung it against Phelim. 'See this, boy? See?' It dated back to the previous century, all dog-eared and stained, half the threads of its spine worn-through and broken. Inside it, written in several different shades of ink, all faded to sepia, were screeds of closely packed gibberish.

'Is it Welsh?' asked Phelim. It was the least insulting thing he could find to say.

'It's what They say. It's what They said to me.' Murdo was speaking in a whisper. His eyes were unnaturally bright and his fingers drummed on the helm. 'What do you make of it? Anything? Can you translate it?'

'Of course not. It's gibberish,' said Phelim, unguardedly.

When at last Murdo turned to look at him, the veins of his eyes were bloodshot. 'But you're a chime child! You're supposed to understand it! *You have to!*' He recovered himself quickly at the sight of Phelim's alarm. 'No matter. Not to fret, son. It's maybe in *hearing* it you can understand.' He snatched back the notebook and fumbled it into a drawer, eyes fixed once more on the horizon. 'Soon be there. Not long now.'

Sweeney stood on the mast's cross-tree, stroking the sole of his foot against its wood. As the light of dawn increased, the sea sent white lozenges of light flickering across his face, and he sang whisperingly under his breath:

'Carts of oak are our ships

Jolly carp are our men . . . When does it rise, Murdo? Is it today for sure, Murdo? Tell us, Murdo.'

'Last week. But this time it rose and it stays risen!' The old man was triumphant. 'There's other trawlermen have seen it. Ignorant lumps: don't know what they're seeing, of course. A new island. They don't realize, and I haven't set them wise. But *I* know. I've seen it every seven year, in the selfsame spot. It rises up, and if a man can throw fire ashore . . . My old granny told me that. Probably never thought I'd take it to heart—must've been six or seven when she told me. But that day she told me, I swore—I'll get out there—to Hy Brasil— and I'll ask them and they'll have to tell me. And they did! They do! It's just that they say it in Faery, and how's a man supposed to . . . S'pose they think it's a great joke: to keep telling me what I want to know, and me still not know it. But this time I'll ask and *you'll* hear what they answer, and comprehend it, and we'll both be richer than Midas! If it hadn't been for the merrows, I'd have it now. I would. I'd have it now.'

Phelim looked over the comfortable, homespun figure of Murdo Jones—collarless shirt, moth-eaten Arran jumper, gabardine trousers which bagged under his rotund belly. None of it seemed in keeping with fairy kingdoms. 'Have what? What is it you wish for?' Above the wake of the boat, seagulls were gathering, dipping and gliding, anticipating the usual litter of fishing.

'Where they hide it, of course. Their Golconda. All their Faery gold. It's somewhere on land. I know that much.'

'Oh, everyone knows that.' Phelim made no attempt to disguise his disgust. 'At the end of the rainbow.' This white-haired, rosy-cheeked, cheery-as-Saint-Nicholas man had let his mind run for sixty years on a fantasy, on fairy tales. Phelim slouched away towards the bow, hands in pockets. Murdo was madder than Sweeney, any day.

'You wait! You see!' Murdo roared after him. 'I'm not talking crocks of gold! I'm talking gold by the ton! Gems! Sea pearls!'

Phelim kicked a pile of ropes. He should have known. Everyone wanted something from him—however absurd, however unlikely, however impossible it was for him to deliver. Everyone wanted Jack o' Green to work some wonder for them. Even though he could hear his sister, plain as plain—'Selfish shellfish, Phee McMe!'—he could not help sinking into a mire of self-pity.

Wishes? Phelim knew what *he* would wish for if the Faeries granted him a wish. Very simple. He would wish the shirt away. He would wish the washerwoman's omen undone. Simple. He would wish not to die.

A gust of wind set the top-hamper tinkling, and Phelim looked round. Sweeney was leaning towards him, grinning loonishly, bare feet clenched around the cross-tree, arms stretched out in supplication. *'Wish the Worm dead!'* He mouthed it, over and over and over again. *'This is our way! Don't you see? You can wish the Worm dead!'*

With a lurch of his seasick stomach, Phelim realized that Hy Brasil was going to be as real as the corn wives, the boas, the Obby Oss, the merrows. Why not? And he was going to be the one to throw fire ashore and make a wish. He could, after all, go on living.

Or he could use the wish to wish the Worm dead.

Phelim kicked the ropes again. What would Sweeney have wished for? To find that swallow with the ruby in its breast?

Or for the Stoor Worm to die? One wish so small, the other so big. There was no knowing. Not gold, though: of that much Phelim was perfectly sure. Again he pictured Sweeney leaping through the spinney of masts, trying to call back the deserter, the traitor, the treacherous Jack o' Green who was running away from his duty. This time all Phelim's hatred was reserved for himself.

A dreary grey sea fret obscured the horizon and any boat that might be sailing by. For all anyone could tell, Hy Brasil was out there now, risen from the sea like a grey seal breaking surface momentarily to look at the shoreline with curious eyes. At any moment, equally, it could sink back down, no one the wiser, no one the richer.

'What good is gold if the world's going to end?' he called out to Murdo over the noise of water and wind.

The lips amidst the snowy beard and moustache were pushed forward in a prodigious pout, and the white brows knit into a scowl. 'You don't want to go believing that witch—nor that fairground freak up there. It won't be the finish of the world. S'only a worm. I've lived 'longside of that Worm all my born days, and it don't circle the world. Nothing like. So what, if it wakes? Britain: what's Britain? Iceland maybe. Scandinavia. Let 'm go. There's other places to live. No Worms in Australia. With that Faery gold, we can make any place a paradise. I know. I planned it. All my days, I've planned how to spend it. And now I've found me a chime child. You're my ticket to Paradise, son. That's what you are.'

They were good words, tenderly spoken; words Phelim had always wanted to hear. And yet his heart continued to trail behind the *May Louisa*. He had a fourth wish just then—not for gold, not for a curse to be lifted, not for the Worm to die, but a fourth, modest little wish. Phelim just wished he were someone else.

*   *   *

103

Like a circular saw cutting along the line of the horizon, the sun came up, a disc buckled out of shape by the weight of rainclouds. Murdo steered towards it, as if towards a lit doorway. As it rose, the rain dispersed. Murdo spread one hand towards the morning star, measuring the sky in spans, and adjusted the helm a degree or two, according to some intuition or secret knowledge.

Phelim craved information. 'Is it big? I mean, does it have mountains and trees? Is it just a rock? How big? Or a sand bank? Maybe we'll hit it! What if we sail right past!'

Sweeney, poised like a tree sloth at the masthead, said: ''Sa great place like the rook in a chess game, but clad all over in brass. Windows like the sterncastles of Tudor galleons, and the waves break against it with never a sound.'

'How do you know it?' snapped Murdo, jealous of his secrets.

'It flies seven green flags,' Sweeney went on, 'and keeps hawks hooded and tied by their feet to perches. Rods and poles and perches. Feet and inches. Tied by their feet and inches . . . *Childe Rolande to the dark tower rode*

Widershins about.

He knocked on the door but nobody came.

Everybody was out.'

'Sweeney has the Knowledge,' Phelim explained. 'He's a marvel.'

'Knowledge be mined and blasted,' said Sweeney, wrapping both arms and legs around the mast in terror. 'I know it because I see it over yonder.'

And there it was—the Isle of Hy Brasil. It must have materialized, rather than risen, for there were no strands of seaweed caught on its crenellations, no streams of seawater drying to a salty slubber. It gleamed like a great cannon barrel aimed at Mars, and its outer harbour wall was a floating boom of barrels and sea chests chained end to end.

The fine sleeting rain returned. It gradually soaked them through, all three. Murdo struck a lucifer but it instantly blew out. He struck another, but fumbled the lamp's latch with his old bony fingers and the match burned down and scorched him. He took out a third.

'No! Don't!' said Sweeney. 'Bad luck to strike three matches in a row.'

'But we must throw the fire! We must!' shouted Phelim, suddenly on the brink of tears. *'What if it sinks down again? What if I can't make a wish?'* He took the box of lucifers from Murdo and, with trembling fingers, struck one, and lit the lantern. It engulfed them in a custard-yellow pool of light.

'Now, who's to throw it?' asked Murdo. 'I would, but it's arthritis I have in my shoulders.'

'I will,' said Sweeney. 'When they shot incendiaries at our ships, we throwed 'em back—phosphor and all. We throwed them further than week-next-Tuesday, I can tell you.'

'No!' said Phelim. 'It must be me. It has to be me.' He could not bear to think of his wish passing to Sweeney or Murdo. 'If you would help me up the mast, Mr Sweeney . . . I can lob it over.'

No one was visible on the brass-walled island—even when Phelim reached the summit of the mast, with the length of cord in his teeth from which swung the lantern. There was no sign of life along the brass parapets or in the mullioned windows. Rigged up like a half-built marquee, a single massive awning of sailcloth flapped over the rooftops of Hy Brasil.

Phelim drew the lantern up after him. 'Gently, gently now,' he heard himself say aloud. He was aware of a foul stench wafting up from the grey, quaggy roadway. Perching on the mast's wooden cross-tree, he took a firm grip on the cast-iron lantern.

Just once, disbelief barged back into his brain, but he

smothered it. 'I wish, I wish, I wish, I wish,' he heard himself whispering. Then he drew back his arm to throw the fire ashore.

He was suddenly aware of a face watching him—a face the shape and texture of a tulip. It took him a moment to identify it, because it was upside down, and the tuft of fine hair hanging down was not a beard but a ponytail. The faery was hanging by his folded legs from a hemp hawser stretched between two pylons—a kind of albino bat shrouded in a crinkling patchwork of dead animals' parts—beetle wings, shed snakeskins, fish-scales, husks. There were no diaphanous tiny wings, no minute bluebell hat. Down below, there were no quaint toadstool homes or miniature palaces. Music hung like a smog over everything, moving restlessly up and down minor scales, never quite coming back to any doh. It raised sadness like a nausea into the back of Phelim's throat.

The expressionless face of the inverted faery looked back at him with dull, white eyes. It was a look so full of contempt that Phelim's shoulders rounded in submission. *'What now, Phee McRabbit?'* he seemed to hear his sister say. But then he thought of his paint-stained, darned and patched flannelette shirt—and flung the lantern in a great arc, over the brass wall and down into the squelching slurry of the streets which, in the early dawn, had no colour but grey. The glass in the lantern broke . . . but the candle did not go out. He had thrown fire ashore on to Hy Brasil!

'I did it! I did it! I did it!' crowed Phelim. 'Now you have to grant me a wish!'

106

11

Hy Brasil

'Is that so now, and is it so?' asked the albino in a voice neither male nor female. 'Then you'd best come ashore with your dish of wishes for the filling.'

Phelim told the others, 'You wait here. I have to go. It has to be me. I'm Jack o' Green, after all.'

Murdo was instantly suspicious, and struggled to make the ship fast, single-handed, so that he too could go ashore. 'Tell 'em to open up their inner harbour, blast 'em!' he called peevishly. Then, when it occurred to him that this might constitute a wish, he hurried to unsay it. 'No! No! Don't! Just tell them: "Murdo and I want to know" . . . you-know-what! "Murdo and I ask: where's your faery hoard?"'

The harbour gates of Hy Brasil remained shut tight. The only way ashore was from the masthead, and Murdo was no longer young enough to climb his own mast. 'Now don't you go forgetting who brought you here, Jack o' Green! Don't you go betraying me!' The pleading desperation in his voice, like a whining mosquito, made Phelim duck his head within his shoulders. But when he saw Murdo struggling to climb the mast, trying to balance on the ship's rail, risking life and limb rather than be left behind, he could not help but feel real pity for him. After so many dogged years surely this old man deserved his dreams to come true. And it was within Phelim's power to make them do so!

Sweeney too (though he looked more terrified than either of them), eyed the wall as if he would jump ashore on to Hy Brasil. Perhaps he was so terrified that his own heartbeat deafened him to Phelim repeatedly saying, 'You stay here. I'll go alone.'

The tulip-faced faery somersaulted down from its rope and started away down the sticky road; Phelim assumed it was leading the way to the royal palace, to the King of Faery. As he followed, the doors of houses opened and other faeries came out to stare. Hy Brasil was not large: the brass wall no more than 100 metres in length. And yet the internal dimensions covered dozens of square miles. The houses were like half eggshells embedded in the clagging ground.

'Are there birds, do you suppose?' Sweeney was saying. 'Do you see birds? Do seabirds see birds? Let me know if you see swallows. Tell me swiftly if you see swifts.'

'Go back to the ship, Sweeney. Please,' said Phelim, desperate to carry through his act of treachery in private, without an audience.

The faery face is incapable of smiling. Phelim mistook their blankness of expression for indifference. They certainly registered no surprise that their island stronghold had been penetrated— only a kind of vacant listlessness, as though they might be a little drunk on the sickly sweet perfume which riddled the place. As the light increased, he could see that the mire at his feet was in fact carmine red.

'Didn't you know? All the blood from all the wars of the world flows down into Otherworld,' said Sweeney, walking bow-legged, on the sides of his feet. He had picked a fine place to touch ground for the first time in a century: he was back at Waterloo, walking in the blood of his comrades. His face was covered in sweat, and his teeth were visible through the yellow thinness of his lips; Phelim could smell the man's fear. So why did he not stay behind in the boat with Murdo? Why did he persist in tagging along?

'You're very afraid, Mr Sweeney,' said Phelim, resorting as he always did to politeness.

108

'And you're not, I suppose?' retorted Sweeney rolling his eyes so that the whites showed.

'I didn't mean . . . I only meant . . . I can manage. I can do this. You don't have to hold my hand. I'm Jack o' Green, aren't I? I'm the one everybody needed.' Saying this, he felt more sure of himself, indispensible. A boy of destiny. Like the rest of this half-sized world of Hy Brasil, it made him feel bigger.

'So you're going to wish for the Worm to die?'

'Of course I am. I said I was, didn't I?'

'No. No, you didn't!'

A wraith-like dog, thinner-waisted than a greyhound, barked at the big strangers, but Phelim stamped his foot at it and it cringed away from him trembling, just as Sweeney was trembling.

'Yea, but even Jack o' Green is open to temptation,' said Sweeney.

The words fell on Phelim like snow off a roof. 'I don't know what you mean,' he spluttered and was instantly, toweringly angry. He used the backs of his hands to cool his burning cheeks. 'What's that supposed to mean? What do you mean? Temptation!'

The street filled up behind them with a dense, whispering crowd of expressionless creatures, their clothes giving no more hint to their sex than their uniformly slender bodies. They were dressed, like caddis flies or hermit crabs, in costumes made up of scavenged bits and pieces. Their hands were all the time reaching out to touch, though their fingers were light as spiders' feet. Sweeney, who had been touched by no one for a hundred years, felt it like the Death-of-a-Thousand-Cuts: there were tears of torment in his eyes. The very sight of him incensed Phelim more than he would have believed possible.

'Look, why don't you go back to the boat, if you're so scared? Why don't you? Nothing's stopping you! Did I ask you to come? I didn't ask you! I don't want you with me. Look at you. *Go back, why don't you?'*

Sweeney stopped so abruptly that the faeries flowed on past him, blue-green like water round an island. He reached out and laid a hand on Phelim's shoulder. 'Because I know what it is to be tempted, boy. I'm a soldier. I know that man Temptation. Don't I live with him in my pocket, come year, go year?'

Phelim turned away and kept walking. He was angry. He was furious. Sweeney waded after him through the faeries. 'I've seen men rob churches, remember! Men stealing off the dead! Men deserting their best friends in battle! Most of all—' His voice rose as Phelim put more distance between them. 'Most of all, son, I know what it is to *want a thing*!'

Phelim began to run. The faeries would not lay hands on Jack o' Green. 'Go back to the boat, Sweeney!'

Sweeney did not have the same immunity, and they pawed him and pinched him and tried to climb up on his shoulders. He yelled: *'You think a madman like me don't crave his wits back?'*

At last Phelim felt compelled to turn and look back. Sweeney was almost submerged in faeries, his umbrella-spoke wings pulled all awry. But he was singing as he sank to the ground:

'The man in the moon came down too soon,

And asked the way to his wits . . . Everyone's got something they'd wish for. What's yours? Gold, is it? Talent? Every one of us!'

Phelim found himself beside a large building. He stepped aside, to get his feet out of the red mire, to get out of reach of Sweeney's voice. He stepped into the atrium of a large public hall, and the door swung round behind him. It shut so tight that he was plunged into darkness, as though the wick of his brain had been snuffed out.

Gradually, his eyes accustomed themselves to the dark.

* * *

'Which of you is the King?' asked Phelim of the hundred faeries who confronted him. They reclined on couches like Romans at a banquet: the entire wall of the circular hall was lined with them: doves roosting in a dovecote. The voice which answered him had a quality of exquisite boredom:

'We have no King. You do so like to impose your own customs on other creatures. That is the arrogance of Mankind. We have no king. No queen. No sheiks or emperors or rajahs.' The faery's ruff of ginger fur bristled with disgust as it spoke the words. Outside, Phelim could hear Sweeney bawling a madman's song:

'*Little Boy Phee*

Says me, me, me

And doesn't know what to ask for . . . '

'Who should I tell my wish to, then?' asked Phelim, trying to master the thumping of his heart.

'*Leave him alone and he'll come home*

With all the gold in Alaska!' sang Sweeney outside.

'You can understand us, then?' said a languishing creature who wore a smell of mould. 'The Seaman has found himself a chime child.'

'I'm sorry?'

'Murdo. The Seaman. With every rising he comes here, asking, wishing, demanding wishes. He understands nothing of our language, but still he comes, every seven years, greedy for wishes.'

Phelim tried to look confident and important; it was not so easy as it had been outside. 'I'm Jack o' Green. Of course I understand you. So you have to grant *my* wish.'

The hundred mould-fluffy creatures on the ledges exchanged glances with each other which might have been mocking if their faces had been less blank. Some even kicked their legs in the air in what might have been fits of mirth.

'It is time to make ready the ships,' murmured one, and

with infinite lethargy ten or twelve rolled off their ledges and fell, like seedcases from a sycamore tree, twirling to the ground. Where their bodies overlapped, their different colours coalesced, like coloured opaque glass. The ruffed ginger creature was among them.

'What about my wish!' Phelim called after him.

A stone-grey child dressed in tinkling strands of seashells turned back. 'Ah yes. Your *wish*.' The whole high atrium hissed like a great seashell with a hundred whispered repetitions: *wish, wish, wish, wish, wish.*

'I threw fire ashore! You have to grant it!' blurted Phelim. Through the wall he could hear Sweeney now simply calling his name, over and over again.

'Ever-Good Green! Ever-Good Jack Green!'

But that *wasn't* his name. He had never asked his parents to call him that, had never known it even had a meaning. And he was *not* good. People only had to ask his sister to know . . . They only had to look inside his head to what he was wishing . . .

'Be true to your friends, Ever-Good Green!' called Sweeney through the wall.

But Phelim wanted to live!

'My wish is that you undo the—' The faery with the ginger ruff continued walking away. 'Wait! Listen!' Phelim ran after him over a floor spongy with mildew and fungi. 'Is it granted? Can you read my mind? Where are you going?'

The faery looked over its shoulder at him, with open contempt. 'Arrogance. Hearken to their arrogance. They truly think the Otherworld exists only for them: three wishes and a pot of gold.' He spat on the floor. 'There are people who think they can buy the Moon's luck by turning over the small change in their pockets, who think they can pilfer each other's luck by snapping a chicken's pelvis. Wishes pishes.'

'But—' Phelim's shoulders rounded. His hands hid up his sleeve-ends.

The faery came stalking back. Even with his eyes shut Phelim could smell the damp, cellarish smell of that grey skin. It pushed its grey face up against Phelim's. 'Did you really suppose that we come back every seven years solely for the joy of *granting wishes to fools?*'

And then their myriad overlapping voices began to mob Phelim like skuas mobbing a puffin:

'We come for a purpose.'

' . . . for our own purposes.'

' . . . reconnoitring.'

'Waiting for the perfect opportunity . . . '

'We were always going to come . . . '

'And now the men are all gone . . . '

' . . . the women will welcome us.'

Their noise filled the room like a rising tide filling a cave. It washed over Phelim making him reel and gibber. But his hands shot out and he grabbed the stone-grey faery by its mouldy pelt. *'Send the Worm back to sleep!'* he yelled. *'That's my wish! Kill it or make it sleep again!'*

The mould came away in his hands.

The faery stared at him. 'The Worm? The Stoor Worm?' Then it began to laugh: the swampy croak of a flabbergasted toad, beckoning for his fellows to revel in the joke. Even as they laughed, their faery faces did not alter. The laughter simply gurgled out of their vacant mouths like water from rigid, shiny taps, and their eyes remained full of smoke.

'Who roused up the Stoor Worm?'

'It was the guns, the thud of the guns!'

' . . . the smell . . . '

' . . . the screams of the dying.'

'Does he think *we* can stop her waking?'

'He has a small mind.'

'Too small to picture the Worm.'

'And he thinks *we* can call off the Hatchlings!'

Phelim bent his knees and curled up in a ball, his arms over his head, his hands over his ears. But their whispered jeers penetrated all the way to his brain.

'Does he think our magic is equal to the Stoor Worm's?'

'Slayer of light.'

'Eater up of the World.'

'Does he think we can raise up a hand and stop the world ending?'

By this time, a hundred small, slim, white hands were raised, translucent, effete and fraily flapping.

'Why are you here, then?' Phelim demanded, kneeling up.

The faery with the ginger ruff of fur cocked his head on one side. 'Ah. He wants a faery story, does he?' he said, voice heavy with sarcasm. 'Once upon a time . . . Isn't that the cage you like to put us in? Very good. A faery story for Jack-o-the-Green . . . Once upon a time, a young female called Michelle de Garis found a faery man sitting under a hedge, and took a liking to him and went with him to Otherworld. She was a rare beauty (for a Human), and we Hidden People wanted brides just like her. So we fought with the men of Guernsey, and some lost and some won, and a sprinkling of wives was taken, but not enough. Never enough. We want more. We always said we would come back for more. So we bided our time. Waited, while the blood spilled down from that "Great War" of yours. Waited till the stones began to hatch and the terror began to spread. Ah, but now . . . *now,* Jack-o-the-Green, the way is open. Think how glad the maids will be of us. What? With nothing but boys and old men to save them from the monsters? So grateful. Ours for the asking. We've come to take brides, that's what. We've come to take brides.'

Its small lower teeth showed ragged behind its lower lip.

Beside that, his face showed nothing of the venom he was speaking, the hatred he and his kind felt towards Humankind who had kept them waiting so long but who stood in their way no longer.

'Our girls will never choose to marry you!' said Phelim, with all the disdain he could muster.

'Did we say we would give them the choice? The girl on your boat, now—the one with no shadow . . . '

At that moment, at the summit of the hall's gigantic roof, a figure too large to be a faery stove in the eggshell dome with the heel of his bare foot. Sweeney, so frightened that he had resorted to climbing the very buildings of Hy Brasil, now deliberately came crashing through the roof, springing from ledge to ledge of the atrium, spoked coatflaps outspread. He spilled faeries from their dirty couches like a bird-nester raiding a cliff, though their mask-like faces registered neither shock nor fright, and they only fluttered to the ground in slow motion.

'We have to get back to the boat!' Phelim said, as Sweeney crash-landed at his feet.

'*I must down to my knees again*

To the coldy breeze and the flies . . . ' sang the madman. 'Where did I hear that? It's modern.' But he did not waste time, as Phelim did, struggling to open the door. He sensibly smashed his way through the eggshell wall of the building and into the street outside.

They ran as if from pursuers, though the faeries around them moved with the treacly slowness of figures in a nightmare. Splashing through all the blood of the Great War, of the Crimean War, of the Boer War, Phelim tried to tell Sweeney, as they ran, the whole miserable extent of his failure.

'They don't grant wishes! It's not true! They can't call off the monsters! I did ask! I swear to God, I asked!' Sweeney would think he had wasted his wish. The others too would think he had asked for gold or fame, or not to die young. They would never believe that he had asked, and that the faeries had refused. 'They want our women! That's why they're here! They've come looking for brides! They want to steal all the girls for brides!' he panted.

'*The Man in the Moon came down too soon,*

To get his poor dog a bone.

When he got there, they were having a war . . .'

'Sweeney! For God's sake! They're invading!'

'Not "for *God's* sake", surely? That would not be in their nature. They are the Undecided Ones—the ones who wouldn't take sides—wouldn't choose between God and Satan when the angels fought. That's who the Faeries are.'

The *May Louisa* lay within the curving arm of the boom, banging its stern dully against the brass walls of Hy Brasil, its sails half furled. But alongside her, miraculously, there lay a second boat! Alexia and the Oss, woken by Sweeney's shouting on the roof, had given chase in a boat half the size of the *May Louisa* and so unseaworthy that they had barely stayed afloat. Now it lay listing drunkenly, banging up against Murdo's boat on the swell, and both Alexia and the Oss had transferred to the *May Louisa* despite everything Murdo had tried to prevent them. At the sight of Phelim, they jumped and shouted and beckoned him down into the boat.

Sweeney ran hoppingly along the brass parapet, indifferent to the prodigious drop on one side, the heaving sea on the other. Phelim followed behind on hands and knees, palms slippery with the cold sweat of terror. The faeries in the street below began to throw things at him—pine cones and boots and fruit furry with the same white mould as they themselves wore. He could hear himself telling them to stop, and not wanting to, because he sounded so grizzling and craven.

Aboard the *May Louisa*, Murdo squinnied up at the two figures on the parapet, and read failure in both faces. Suddenly,

116

without warning, Mad Sweeney leapt out over thin air—a leap of ten or twelve feet, to grasp the head of the mast.

'Did he find out?' Murdo called. 'Did the boy find out about my gold?'

'They wouldn't grant his wish! They wouldn't grant it!' Sweeney whispered the answer, tears crawling down his wrinkled cheeks, his nose running. Raising the sleeve of his coat to wipe his face, Sweeney left it there, hiding his eyes. Perhaps just hiding. 'They wouldn't . . . ' he mumbled.

Instantly Murdo began to cast off. His old fingers tugged at the rolling-hitch tying the boat's painter to the quay. It came undone at once.

'What are you doing, Uncle?' demanded Alexia. 'You can't leave Phee!' She and the Oss came at him, trying to stop him pushing off. Murdo cursed them, ignored them. They shouted at him to wait for Phelim, stranded up there on the brass wall, but the *May Louisa* drifted out from the floating-quay anyway.

'They've had me once. Do you think I mean to go down there again? Not for nobody.'

Alexia struggled with him as he unfurled the sail, struck out at him as he made fast the down-haul, screamed at him as he close-hauled the sheets, but the rattling flap of the sail drowned her out.

Phelim was standing up on the top of the wall now, a hail of missiles pelting him, making him stagger.

'Jump! Jump!' yelled Alexia.

'Jump on to me, Phee!' yelled the Oss spreading its skirts.

'Jump!' called Sweeney, beckoning Phee across the widening gap.

Suddenly, with a slicing of great horsy teeth hidden away in some odd part of his horsy anatomy, the Oss bit clean through the sheet securing the lateen sail. It swung round, making everyone aboard duck, and dislodging Sweeney from the mast. For a moment, the sail filled in such a way that the *May Louisa* was driven backwards against the breakwater.

Within the perimeter wall, the faeries, in their slow, lazy, communal way of doing things, had fetched brooms and spars and washing-line props and were throwing them like javelins at Phelim Green. Casually, almost indifferently, they were trying to knock him off the wall for the sport of it. A bamboo cane struck him end-on in the calf; he was amazed how much it hurt. Phelim saw that he would never have another chance. He crouched down (as he had seen Sweeney do) and sprang into the loose-flapping canvas of the sail. It was like jumping into the awning of a shop: he slid down and off, the canvas burning the skin of his wrists and ankles, and landed on top of the Oss who had spread himself like a fireman's jump-sheet.

Swearing in Welsh, Murdo grabbed hold of the snaking broken rope-end, and, catching the wind once more, got the *May Louisa* away into open water, just before fireballs started flying over the brass parapets of Hy Brasil and plopping with noisy hisses into the sea. Looking back, Phelim could see silhouette after silhouette, thin-hipped, large-headed, rag-shaggy creatures pulling themselves up on to the wall and signalling their ill-wishes in slow, obscene gestures. The second, listing boat was already on fire.

A moment or so later, the great brass gates to the interior harbour swung open and a Faery fleet of golden craft began to issue out, like notes emerging from an organ pipe.

Back at the beginning of the world, the Faeries might have been Undecided about whether to side with Good or Evil: now they were in no such quandary. Now they were single-mindedly bent on gaining their desire: wives to enjoy during the last remaining days of the World.

12

High Water

Murdo was silent, struggling with the idea that Hy Brasil rose not to grant wishes but like an enemy submarine to scan its target. The Oss, turning round and round on the deck, was a dripping black capstan.

The Faeries gave no impression of hurrying: their movements were as havering as earthworms. And yet, like worms in earth, they infested every cubic yard of air. They took great care never to touch the water—did not even coil the trailing ropes of their ships, for fear the salt water wetted them. They swarmed aboard in such number that their fleet *should* have wallowed deck-deep—and yet their no-weight made no impression on the frail little craft. No orders were shouted, but they worked amorphously, like termites who think as one while performing individual tasks. And their purpose was not to pursue Phelim or Murdo or Sweeney who had merely spurred them into action. The moment had come for them to invade, as they had planned to do all along. The time was ripe for invasion.

'They want human brides!' Phelim tried to explain to the others in the boat, jerking a shirt cuff in the direction of the Faery fleet. 'They don't grant wishes; all that's just a story! They've always been going to come! They were just waiting their chance. Now they know there's no menfolk to fight them off, so they're coming after brides . . . !'

At that moment, the Faeries loosed off a volley of golden arrows at the *May Louisa*, with no more effort than a rabble of schoolboys throwing sweet wrappers over a wall. The arrows flew over with dreamlike slowness, glittering like strands of gossamer. Everyone ducked for shelter—behind the mast, beneath the wheelhouse.

Murdo, though, was too distraught to stay hidden. He stood up again, shaking both fists. 'No, no! They got no right! Granting wishes, that's what Faeries do!' he sobbed, slapping a hand to his neck, as if to swat a mosquito.

The Obby Oss began dancing: jeering and showing its tail to the ships behind, his instinct to whirl and jig triggered by the mention of invasion. *'Steal our women? Steal our women! No Cornishwoman would take you!'* he bawled over the stern.

Mad Sweeney returned, liked a crazed gibbon, to the mast's cross-tree, where he clawed a seagull out of the air and ripped open its chest before its wings had even stopped beating. All his old insanity had come flooding back. He groped inside the seagulls ribs and peered into its chest-cavity, then flung it aside in disgust. His heel banged against the tautness of the sail so that it resounded like a drumskin.

It was Alexia who noticed that Murdo's nose was bleeding. 'Are you hurt, Uncle?'

Phelim watched revolted as the dead seagull drifted astern on the wake. Sweeney sang:

'Cry baby bunting,
Daddy's gone a-hunting,
Gone to buy a dragon skin
To wrap a little Sweeney in . . . '

For a long time they stared up at him hunched like a vulture above them, his eyes streaming tears:

'Hark, hark the sky's all dark;
The Stoor Worm's coming to town.
Hark, hark the cats do bark;
The world is burning down!'

'Should'a found out about the gold,' mumbled Murdo. 'Should've.'

Phelim did not even look round. 'What use is gold, if the

world's going to end?' he said irritably. And yet he already understood. The End of the World was too big a thing to fit inside anyone's head. It stayed outside, remained unreal: just words. Phelim, for example, kept worrying what his sister would say about his torn clothes, his dirty hands, the glashans in the living room. If the world was going to end, what did it matter? What did any of it matter? And yet the worries did not go away.

'Uncle?' said Alexia. 'Uncle Murdo, are you all right?'

One moment he was standing beside her, a hand on her arm, the next he was sinking to the deck, his legs buckling as if made of something too soft and spongy to bear his weight. His jaw struck the ship's rail, so that his head was bent backwards, face-up to the sky.

It took them a long time to find the shiny arrowhead embedded in his neck; it was only as large as a needle. Around the wound, a large black bruise was spreading. 'He will be all right, won't he?' asked Alexia.

Murdo was muttering, though his eyes were shut: there were ropes to be shortened, ropes to be let out; the sails were rumbling, hungry for wind. The others squatted round him anxiously. Even Sweeney was drawn down to the ship's rail, his fists in his hair:

'*Home is the hunter, home from the sea*
And the sailor home from the hill.'

'Shut up, Sweeney!' shouted Phelim, then turned on Alexia. 'Isn't there some magic? I thought you were supposed to be a witch? Don't you know any magic?'

But she only curled herself into a smaller and smaller ball, saying her uncle's name.

The Faery fleet was overhauling them now, spreading out into a crescent as slender as a new moon, half encircling the *May Louisa*. Another shower of arrows floated over, carried like thistledown on the wind. Wherever one pierced the ship there was a pulpy darkening of the wood, like apples bruising. The empty sail rattled over their heads.

'Over the side with him!' said the Oss. 'He's gone.'

Phelim slapped out at him, but Sweeney agreed. 'He's right, Phelim. One that dies at sea must be buried at sea. That's the rule.'

'Sea will come after its own, else!' whimpered the horse in self-defence. He spread his valance of skirts over Murdo's face, and rocked forward and back, forward and back. 'You'z'll have plenty sea pearls to richen you down there,' he confided to the lifeless man.

Without Phelim's help, they began to lift Murdo, in order to heave his body over the side. There was a delay while Alexia found net-weights enough to stop the body floating.

'Him's only a week or two ahead of us all,' said the Oss, in a low, sombre voice, 'with the Worm a-waking.'

One of Murdo's shoes swung against the wood bulwark with a sharp inappropriate bang. It sounded like a door slamming.

And suddenly Phelim remembered a door slamming somewhere else, far off in his childhood—of his sister shutting something or someone out—saying over her shoulder, *'Get to bed, Phee McBaby and stop your grizzling. He's gone now, and good riddance to bad rubbish.'*

'Stop,' he said.

His voice was so altered that the others looked back at him, the dead man dangling fore and aft over the ship's rail. 'Stop,' said Phelim again. 'I still need his help.'

'Help? What to do? To do what?'

'To hold off the Faeries,' said Phelim. Sweeney's eyes narrowed like a hawk and he laid a restraining hand on the body to prevent it tilting into the sea. 'First the Faeries and then the Stoor Worm,' Phelim went on. They stared at him and were slow to move. Around them the gilt pins of the Faery archers cankered the fishing boat with blooms of mould.

'Well? I'm Jack o' Green, aren't I?' said Phelim squaring his shoulders. 'Do as I tell you.'

They pulled the body inboard without another word. It fell to the deck with an almighty thud which made them all blink.

By keeping the sails full, they managed to stay ahead of the Faery fleet, trimming the *May Louisa* as if it were a treasure ship pursued by privateers. There was a strong following wind as well.

They would have liked to return the way they had come, but without Murdo at the helm, the current and the rising tide carried them back along the coast. To their dismay, they saw much of their laborious journey cross-country being undone; it was like sliding down the snake on a snakes-and-ladders board. It would take them a day just to recover lost ground.

The beach they sighted first was backed by empty sand dunes. Sweeney was in favour of sailing on until they reached some harbour or jetty, but Phelim said there was no time: they must run the *May Louisa* ashore.

'Wreck uz ship, you mean?' The Oss turned round twice, tangling his own hooves in the ropes. The keel whistled, then grated, then touched bottom with a thud which pitched them all on to the deck.

'High tide, you said.'

'None higher,' said Sweeney.

'How much higher will this one be than the last? Show me.' The previous high water mark was clearly defined by a rime of seaweed, litter, and salt. Sweeney cleared it in a single leap, landing amid an explosion of sand. They had roped Murdo's feet together, flies gathering over them as they worked, like black, prying little faeries. Now the old man lay in the surf, each wave lending him an impression of life, lifting his head and hands. The sea too was tasting the clammy tang of his skin.

'Drag him into the dunes!' said Phelim. 'Right up there—and quickly. Quickly!'

It was the turn of the others to protest. Those who died at sea must be buried at sea: that was the law of the oceans. But Phelim insisted, and with such unassailable certainty that they obeyed, the Oss spinning and cavorting, Alexia silently crying, Sweeney rending at songs as he did at birds, pulling them in pieces:

'Hearts of coke are our ships.
Oily tarred are our men.
We always are buried . . . '

With stubs of driftwood and with their bare hands, they scooped a shallow grave among the sand dunes, and all the while the Faery fleet was crowding into the bay, carried on the same rising tide, following the same shortest route to landfall. They would swarm off their ships, small and deadly as plague rats: gangplanks were protruding already from each bow. The keels touched bottom soundlessly, as light as coconut shells.

'White sand and grave sand
Who'll buy my white sand!
Who'll buy my grave sand!' sang Sweeney.

The soft dunes made the movements of the burial party as slow as those of the Faeries, for it sucked at their feet, plucking off their shoes. They waded knee-deep in sand. Sweeney was green with terror, but when Phelim began covering over Murdo's body, Sweeney followed suit, scrabbling sand between his legs like a dog burying a bone.

'Will you not say a word for him, Phee? Not a word? What he did? He took you out there to make a wish! He got killed trying to help us! He's a hero!' Alexia was choking on a mixture of sorrow, fright, and anger, appalled at this unseemly funeral for the uncle she imagined had died in a noble cause.

124

Phelim shot a warning glance at Sweeney; a look which said, *'Not a word. Not one word of what he said.'*

'All right,' panted Phelim, spitting sand. 'Let this be his epitaph: "He saved our women and girls from the Faeries". He would have wanted to do that, eh, Sweeney? He was very . . . worried for Alexia's sake. Isn't that right?'

'Yes, yes!' said Sweeney. 'Yes, yes, yes, yes, yes, yes!'

'Wanted her kept safe from the Faeries.' His hair, his eyebrows, his shirt were all crusty with sand. It was impossible to read the expression on his face. 'Now help me bury him, will you?'

As the last tuft of white beard was hidden from sight, the first Faeries fluttered down on to the sand from their galleons—as slow to drop as shreds of torn paper or flower petals.

Sweeney set off to run, the soft sand hampering him, like a man running in a nightmare. 'They'll take me down below; shut my soul in a lobster pot! I'm not brave like you, Ever-Good!'

'Faeries are not merrows,' Phelim called after him. 'Don't you see how careful they are to keep themselves dry?'

It was true. Not one jumped down into the surf (as fishermen would in beaching a boat). Not one came ashore but did so dry-shod, kicking up a little spurt of dry sand, infinitely careful not to be wetted by surf or spray. There were so many of them, congregated in such a small expanse of sand, that they took on the vileness of an ant swarm or woodlice unearthed from a log.

The Oss and Alexia wanted to run, too—to get away, to run inland—to raise the alarm, perhaps, shouting through village streets, 'Get your women away! Hide your women and girls! The Faeries are coming for them! The Faeries are coming!'

Sweeney yearned for the deep, dark forest.

But Phelim hunkered down beside the sandy grave, knotted

his fists in the coarse marram grass, and watched the Faeries land, with the intensity of a wild animal watching its prey. Alexia was the first to kneel down beside him again. 'What are we doing, Phee? What are we waiting for?'

Phelim did not answer. He was busy talking to some invisible adversary, muttering under his breath. 'Come on, then. Come for him. Come and take him, if you want him. Come and get him, why don't you?'

The rising tide shifted the Faery fleet into disarray, turning its keels this way and that. The Faeries were climbing the beach, now—too light to sink into the soft sand, too certain of their success to hurry. But behind them the tide kept rising, each large wave spilling higher and higher, each wave arching its back like an angry cat. The sea was filling up: like a sink filled to overflowing, it was brimming higher and higher, pulled by the drag of the moon but seething, also, with a wrath of its own.

Phelim jumped to his feet. *'Come on then! He's here! Come and get him!'* Alexia dragged on the tail of his shirt, thinking he was calling out to the Faeries, challenging them to a battle. But Phelim was talking to the Sea.

And the Sea had heard him.

It was coming—coming to fetch back its rightful prize— the body of Murdo who had died at sea. It turned over the seaweed, re-absorbed the salty high-water mark. It heaved on up the beach towards the dunes and the fisherman's dry grave.

Faeries adept at dodging ripples and splashes, found themselves overtaken now by large, shouldering waves as big as tanks, cut off by tendrils of foamy water reaching into the dunes. Large, leaping waves, urged on by the wind, swamped them, leaving them first shocked by cold, next floundering out of their depth. Their mould (which seemed more skin than clothing) dissolved away in the brine, and whereas gravity

126

had little hold on them, water overpowered them as it would a moth, a butterfly, a gnat.

Their expressionless faces showed no fear, no horror, no distress, but a high, almost ultra-sonic whistling scream clamoured in Phelim's head, while the others covered their ears.

All of a sudden, the dunes were too dangerous a place to be. Phelim jumped up and the little party of friends scattered, running full tilt as the sea over-topped the beach and came slopping through the dunes, seeking out Murdo's body.

'Run!' cried Phelim and they ran, the sea piling over the dunes, scummy with drowned Faeries. The leading waves gouged into the sand, scooping it up into a glittering soup; the sea was digging for Murdo like a hyena scenting a hidden carcass, rooting it out, grubbing it up. Through the translucent banks of vengeful water they saw the old man unearthed, legs washed free, rolled on to his back by the undertow, for all the world as if he were asleep in a hammock of water.

Then he was gone. The sea had taken its due, invading the land as far as it needed, to grab its rightful spoils. When it had fallen back to high-water mark, the sandy beach was new minted, gold, unblemished, empty.

Phelim went back among the dunes. A hollow imprint survived tracing the outline of the missing body. Phelim planted his hand where Murdo's head had lain and made a swirl in the sand. 'I will do it now, thanks to you,' he said. 'I will stop the Worm waking.'

The others stared at him, this altered, confident Green Man of theirs. He flicked the sandy hair out of his eyes.

'Well? I'm Jack o' Green, aren't I? That's what you fetched me here to do, isn't it? To stop the Stoor Worm waking.'

In the face of their obvious doubts, he wilted a little. 'I have to try, at least.'

13

The Last Sheaf

Inland, everything was changing because of the Hatchlings.

Sucking pigs roasted on village greens. Brass bands played 'Sommer is y-comen in', and morris dancers polished up their repertoire of dances. Rumours of mythical monsters and unexplained phenomena had sent people scurrying back to the 'Old Ways'—all they remembered of their grandparents' quaint beliefs and practices.

When the zany procession of Green Man, Maiden, and Madman walked into a village—(they left the Oss to bypass the towns, for fear he was mistaken for a Hatchling)—they were greeted with cheers and drinks of cider, with songs and sandwiches and stories of local wonders.

But the rites were all a bit tame—all a bit self-conscious. The majority of people were still looking for a rational explanation: reapers massacred, farm beasts savaged, rumours of monsters and alien invaders . . . Some thought the Germans must be behind it, or demobbed soldiers come home pistol-happy from the trenches. Alexia saw it in their faces.

She saw, too, that there was no point in warning them what was in store. Their small, polite, twentieth-century imaginations would never come to grips with Evil on the scale of the Stoor Worm: the World-Eater, Devourer of Time and Place. Corn dollies and folk-songs: that was their idea of the Past.

She saw, too, how Phelim swallowed down the cheers and the cider. He loved the crowns of laurel given him by horticultural ladies in summer frocks, the ribbony cloaks they made him out of green crêpe paper, the welcoming speeches, the plates of free roast pork. It was fun. It was festive. It was flattering. 'If these are the Old Ways, I like them!' he said, laughing and holding out his plate for more.

Out in the countryside, the harvest which Phelim had started to reap under a hot August sun was now mostly cut and garnered into barns. But in one field they passed, on their way back to meet the Oss, reaping had only just come to an end. A single tussock of wheat still stood, like a tuft of beard missed by a man shaving.

'Want to earn yourself a sixpence, son?' The face emerging from behind the wall made them both jump.

'What, ratting?' Sometimes, when the last sheaf in a field was cut, the rats marooned within it broke for freedom while the reapers came after them with flails and sticks.

'Nay. Cut the last sheaf for us. Us hands all raw from sickling, but you, you could finish him off, no hardship. Big strong lad like you.'

Phelim was flattered. He had not been much good with a sickle, but there was so little left to reap—only enough for one last sheaf. Not enough to hide a corn wife or the Noonday Twister, he was sure of that.

'Be careful, Phee,' said Alexia under her breath, but where was the danger in reaping a sheaf of wheat? Phelim climbed over a stile into the field. Scrambling over after him, Alexia wished they had gone to meet with the Oss first. Someone handed Phelim a sickle, and drew back into the circle of men which had formed spontaneously around the tussock of wheat.

'These men aren't tired,' hissed Alexia in his ear. 'Look at them. Why are they asking you?'

'Perhaps they're scared of rats,' said Phelim with a touch of bravado. To tell the truth, he was not fond of rats himself. His sister had once locked him in the cellar for dropping a cup, and he had stood up all night, imagining rats in the darkness. Still, he was Phelim Jack o' Green, and the fate of the world rested on his shoulders. He would hack down this dismal tatter of wheat as a rehearsal for killing the Stoor Worm. The magic in him would keep the rats at bay.

The ripe wheat hissed at him; the yellow ears trembled with outrage as he sheared them through. But no rats rushed out squealing. The nest of a harvest mouse hung precariously from a single stalk; Phee dislodged it and passed it to Alexia to hold. Then he finished the job. Soon the wheat lay like spillikins, hugger mugger along the ground. He gathered it into a sheaf, and a reaper handed him a length of twine to bind it with.

'Him 'as killed it,' said a voice behind him.

'Him 'as,' agreed another.

When Phelim turned round, every reaper had raised his sickle to his chest. Their expressions were of feigned outrage, pretended anger.

'But you *told* him to!' protested Alexia.

'It's the Old Way,' said a boy too young to have even served in the Great War. 'Grandad said. It's the Old Way.'

'A life for a life,' said another, wiping his dry lips with a sleeve.

'Him's killed the spirit of the field. Now the spirit's got to be paid. In blood.'

'Don't be ridiculous,' said Phelim, but it was not the right response to men who had keyed themselves up to commit murder. They had fallen back on the bloody ways of their ancestors.

They formed a paling fence around their sacrificial beast, excluding Alexia. The hot excitement gripping their bowels made them feel more vital and alive, convincing them still further that Old Magic was at work.

'But I'm Jack o' Green!' piped Phelim. 'I'm needed, to kill the Stoor Worm! Tell them, Alexia! I'm the Green Man!'

130

A sickle whistled and struck the sheaf clutched to his chest. He turned around and around, trying to protect his undefended back. Everywhere he was confronted by muzzy, unfocused eyes, top lips beaded with sweat, tongue tips protruding with intent concentration.

'Don't,' said Phelim. 'Please!' He heard a blade cut through the gristly air and turned to intercept the blow with the sheaf in his arms. The crescent of the sickle cut through the twine, and the Last Sheaf disintegrated at Phelim's feet with a noise like a sigh.

'Unite and unite and let us all unite
For summer is a-come unto today . . . ' The singing came over the wall like a stray tennis ball and landed among them.

'And whither we are going we will all unite
In the merry morning of May!'

The black, conical tip of the Obby Oss appeared above the drystone coping and, climbing the stile, it began to dance and caper along the very ridge of the wall, scattering slate-stone to right and left.

'You have a shilling in your purse; I wish it were in mine,
In the merry morning of May!'

Then it leapt into the field and came skipping and twirling over the stubble, raising gleanings and harvest dust in golden clouds under its hooves.

The reapers, uncertain what they were seeing, flung their sickles wildly in the direction of the flapping black shape and fled, the excitement in their bellies turning to watery terror as the Oss's strange snickering laughter pursued them all the way home.

Phelim picked himself up, brushed the dust off his clothes. His knees were gibbering as he flung his arms around the Oss in gratitude.

'So, Green Jack. Do you still like the Old Ways?' said Alexia.

'Oh, I've been more scared than that,' he answered airily.
' . . . But only of my sister.'

Thanks to the *May Louisa* carrying them so far out of their way, the town of Storridge lay once more in their path. They would have to pass through it a second time. But Storridge was surely so respectable that it would scarcely even have noticed the strange things happening round about. Once a year, at the Summer Fête, it might just lay aside the Twentieth Century like a lilac cardigan and indulge in cheese-rolling or pig-racing or weaving corn-dollies. But as for blood sacrifices . . . Alexia and Phelim laughed about it, envisaging the manageress of the cafeteria scowling over her spectacles at a convention of druids, taking their orders for tea and scones.

'Imagine! They live on the Worm's back and they don't even know it!' Alexia laughed.

Phelim came to a halt. 'Live on its back? What do you mean?' Unconsciously, he raised himself on to the balls of his feet so that his heels came off the ground.

'Of course. Why d'you think it's called Storridge? Stoor Ridge—the Stoor Worm's neck: that's what it would have been once—back in the days when they told the story of Assipattle. See that mountain right on the horizon? That's this bit at the top of the spine.' She patted herself between the shoulders. 'And where the town is? That's the ridge of its neck, where the mane would grow on a lion.'

Phelim stared at her. He looked at the ground he was standing on; it was not scales or hide, but clinkered roadway. How could you build on a dragon without waking it? How could you lay roads over its tail and flanks and shoulders, plough the earth covering it, grow crops and graze animals, drive buses and gallop horses without waking it? He looked at the outcrops of grass-covered earth but by no stretch of the imagination could he see a sleeping dragon. At least . . . nothing living could be so big. It defied imagination.

After a few moment's frantic effort to size up his opponent, this enemy against which he was pitted, Phelim gave up. He found he was slightly less afraid. Something which is too big to see is too big to be frightening, because it does not fit inside your head.

Phelim and Alexia agreed that they should not draw attention to themselves in Storridge, so as to be quickly through it and out the other side. After all, they had lost two precious days. And tomorrow Phelim would have to fight and kill the Stoor Worm.

Even Assipattle had not managed that, and Assipattle was a myth.

14

Burning the Bush

When they heard it first, they thought maroons were firing for a ship in distress. But then, as they got close to the town, they could make out the insistent rhythm of a drum—of several drums—all beating out the same lopsided tattoo. There was singing, too, weaving in and out between the houses, up and down the steep Georgian terraces, muffled momentarily by buildings, swelling out again into an open space. Oily, smoking torches created an orange aura over the heads of the procession and lit the white of their clothing, though not their faces. Dozens upon dozens of men and women and children were herding through the streets singing the repetitive strains of something with five beats to the bar and a top G fit to break glass.

Many of the men were drunk, and many of the children were in night-clothes, dragged from their beds to join in the progress round the town, eyes starry and cheeks feverish with sleep. The fringes of the crowd reeled outwards occasionally, then plunged back into the pack, cannoning singers against one another. For a moment, between ending the song and starting it again, there was a breath-stopping pause in which the only sound was of a hundred feet tramping, still keeping time. Then the drums would thunder in again and the song would wind its way up and down the scale as the marchers wound their way up and down the streets.

At close quarters, the drum beat reverberated through Phelim's very ribcage until he felt his heart stagger. It was marvellous! Was this really Storridge, where he and Alexia had taken tea amid the suffocating calm of respectable gentlefolk? Yes, there was a gang of waitresses from the cafeteria. And there was the supervisor, her hair unpinned, wearing one of her lace tablecloths as a shawl. Other dancers were in skimpy, oblong shifts of sheeting or sateen pulled on over their sensible cardigans or best demob suits. They might have looked druidical but for the puckered seams and tacked hemlines.

The Obby Oss was entranced. He began to dance and spin in time to the music, leaping and pouncing. This was one town where they would know him for what he was! At the sight of him dancing out of the dark, the crowd drew back, concertinaed, those at the back last to spot the two-legged horse. Their eyes rounded with fright, the children hid behind their mothers, some of the women screamed. But then, with his mad capering and dizzy cavorting, the Oss somehow conveyed his good-nature, and the crowd opened up to take him and his companions to heart.

Storridge had seen its fair share of Hatchlings since the day Phelim and Alexia took tea there. Redcaps had roosted in the church belfry; a nuckelavee had dragged its transparent bag of guts into the lee of the bus-shelter. Merrows had stolen souls from the boatyard, and just today the remains of faeries, like drowned squabs, had washed up in the storm drain. Church and State had done nothing to help, the Vicar of St Matthew's insisting people were in the grip of communal hysterics, the Police closing down all the pubs, then shutting themselves up inside the Police Station.

Only one man had come to the rescue. He was heading the crowd now, holding, for a wand-of-office, a tutti-pole made of florist's bouquets nailed to a broom handle: the man who had undertaken to redeem the town from peril and confusion: Mr Pringle the librarian.

Mr Pringle, whose scoliosis and asthma had kept him out of the wartime trenches, was leading his troops now against the powers of darkness. He had trawled his library for books on every aspect of folklore and demonology. He had rediscovered rituals and rites so old that even the oldest inhabitants did not recall them. He had identified the monsters with all the meticulous care of a bird-watcher or a trainspotter. Mr Pringle had re-invented Old Ways which had never even been practised in Storridge. In his white shirt and cricket trousers, in his straw boater bound round with long green ribbons, Mr Pringle had taken on a virility and authority no one had ever suspected in him. And the very transformation of Mr Pringle from rabbit to magician seemed in itself part of his Magic.

He had given orders for the Police to be locked in their own cells, for the town boundaries to be beaten with hazel twigs, for the choirboys to wear bishops' mitres. He had commissioned the Mothers' Union to make 'witch-bottles' to fend off evil, and to weave corn dollies. He had organized the big, rough boys to go out stoning wrens, and he had daubed blood on the lintels of public buildings. Ox blood, he said. He had called for the schoolteacher to be pelted with ink pellets and pebbles by his pupils, for iron horseshoes to be nailed up at every door, and for bonfires to be lit at either end of the High Street. In short, he had let loose superstition in the genteel borough of Storridge, and like those Spaniards who let bulls loose to run through the streets, had delivered the town into a state of frenzied, terrified joy.

Even Mr Pringle had been unnerved by the sight of the Obby Oss, black and headless and spinning like a top on its spindly legs. He watched it now, leading his Children of Hamelin helter-skelter through the ornamental flowerbeds of the Jubilee Memorial Park, rushing at the women, making them shriek and giggle under his valance of black skin. But if Mr Pringle's confidence in his book-knowledge faltered, he very soon recovered himself. As the procession milled past a public house, he ripped down the notice outside: CLOSED BY ORDER OF THE POLICE, and pushed open the door. 'Cider for the Luck-Bringer!' he declared, unable, without his reference books, to give a correct name to the Obby Oss. 'And cider for his grooms!'

'Oh, he is not my groom!' panted the Oss, already drunk on the music and the drumming.

'Oss, hush,' said Alexia, but the Oss was off chasing the café supervisor in and out of the tables, spilling glasses of cider as fast as they were served. His flapping flanks absorbed the spills, ingesting whole pints as fast as if he had a head to sup with. 'This is not my groom!' the Oss persisted. 'This is the hero of the hour! Victor over the Outlanders! Caller up of the Sea! Wisher of Wishes!'

'Oss!' snapped Phelim.

'Yes, don't prattle, Oss,' said Alexia, moving smartly to his side, grabbing a fistful of ribbons.

The Oss shrugged her off. 'What? What's wrong! These people here understand the Old Ways! Look at them! Hearken to the accordion! That drumming!' While the drums beat, he was physically incapable of standing still. The flat disc of his body heaved and flexed; he ducked and curtsied in time to the tune. 'Never fear, my fellows! Here comes Jack o' Green with his Maiden and his Oss and his Fool! Here comes the Green Man to stop the Stoor Worm waking!'

'Oss!' moaned Phelim.

The noise in the pub did not abate. Most did not even catch the Oss's words. But Mr Pringle did. They saw him jerk upright on his stool, his face register the words like a bird-watcher registering the sudden appearance on his lawn of an osprey or a dodo. Phelim saw the eyes behind their thick lenses study him, that precise, orderly mind toy with the possibility that here was Jack o' Green, the ultimate Bringer of Good.

'Born under the stroke of midnight!' the Oss lumbered on, speech slurring as the cider reached some cortex within his headless body. 'Tomorrow he will vanquish the Worm izzelf. Then we'll have zomething to dance about!'

'Jack o' the Green,' said Mr Pringle, cleaning a stain off the table in front of him, his finger wrapped in a clean white handkerchief. 'Is he now? An honour indeed. Indeed. A cider for Jack, Miss Griggs, if you would be so kind, and one each for his companions.'

A sudden presentiment of disaster made Alexia get up to leave, but Phelim was flattered. His sister had never allowed him so much as a sweet sherry at Christmas—*'Aren't you enough like your father already, Phee McFish?'* Now that he sipped it, he liked the taste of the golden liquor. When Mr Pringle asked him—'Won't you bless us in the Old Way, Master Jack?'—Phelim only shrugged and grinned and ducked his face shyly to the glass again.

'Phelim, *we have to be going*. Remember?' Alexia hissed in his ear. 'Tomorrow Stoor Head.' But already Mr Pringle was organizing his *pièce de résistance*, his *coup de théâtre*, his climax to a splendid day's paganism.

'A blessing!' said Mr Pringle climbing on to the table. 'Mr Jack o' Green is here to give us his blessing!'

'Bless you,' mumbled Phelim, embarrassed. But that was not quite what Mr Pringle had in mind.

An hour later, the Bush was ready: a bale of straw with a pitchfork deeply embedded in it. The procession had adjourned from the pub to the bonfire at the top of the High Street. It was two in the morning, and Phelim felt pasty with weariness, nauseous from his first ever quart of cider. His limbs shook, though the heat from the bonfire was scorching his cheeks.

'I don't think . . . ' he kept starting to say. 'Tomorrow I have to . . . ' But the town belonged to Basil Pringle tonight, to the Master of the Revels.

Though the drums beat on, the Obby Oss had at last stopped dancing. He ran to and fro, arguing the folly of Pringle's idea. 'There are better ways than fire! Dancing and music, why not? Not fire.'

But Mr Pringle was confident of his facts. 'For centuries it was done every year. The Burning of the Bush—not just here, but all over . . . A Burning Bush carried from end to end of the town.'

'But the town was half its length then!' protested Alexia.

'Ah, but we hadn't the *real* Jack o' Green in those days, either.' Mr Pringle grinned at his argument. 'Only men, dressed up!'

'*Men*, yes! Not boys!' cried Alexia, pushing Phelim in front of him. 'He's only a boy, look!'

It was true Pringle would never have press-ganged a local into performing this feat; his neighbours might look unkindly on him for injuring a member of his own library. But an outsider—especially an outsider claiming magical powers— was the perfect material for Mr Pringle's Grand Finale. As he wedged petrol-soaked rags into the bale of straw, Basil Pringle no longer cared whether the boy with the freckle-splattered face was the real Jack o' Green or not; anticipation burned in his stomach like hot plum brandy and his hands shook with excitement. Not since the opening night of the Storridge Players' *Charley's Aunt* had he felt such a surge of adrenalin.

The odd, circular, headless horse barged up against him and almost knocked him off his feet, but Phelim arrogantly, drunkenly insisted: '*It's all right!* I can do this.'

It embarrassed him to see Alexia and the Oss talking about him as if he were their own personal property, worse still as if he were helpless. The cider had fuddled him, but it also made him confident he could perform this ancient rite for the

139

people of Storridge—that it was within his powers—that it was his duty, no less. How difficult could it be, after all?

'It's only straw,' he said.

'He lied. The Obby Oss lied,' Alexia told the librarian. 'This isn't Green Jack. He's nobody. Just a boy.'

'That's easily remedied,' said Mr Pringle bubbling over with high spirits. 'He shall have greens to wear like the old mummers!' And before Phelim could protest, he was handing his shirt to Alexia and being festooned with strips of cloth, viny clematis ripped off the house-fronts, the raffia fly-curtain from the pub's doorway. From the crown of his head to his boots, they draped him—not so much dressing as decorating him, obliterating his real identity under a costume that hid his face, his hands, his colouring. They made him as anonymous as a Ku Klux Klansman, as androgynous as a scarecrow.

'He must not come to harm,' said the Oss. *'Too much depends on him!'*

'Quiet,' said Phelim. 'I can do this.'

'You see?' said Mr Pringle. 'Jack is ready and willing. So let the Bush be Burned, and let Jack o' the Green purge us with fire and bless us with ash!'

The fishmonger from Sheep Street and the oculist from Bunn's Lane managed to turn the bale over and lift it in the air impaled on the pitchfork. They put the wooden handle into Phelim's hands, resting it against his shoulder like a rifle. He staggered under the prodigious weight—a hundredweight of straw.

Then the crowd was all round him—men, women, and children—all striking Lucifer matches on the pavement or walls and throwing them upwards at the bale. Some of them missed.

'We must not lose him now,' whispered the Oss, thinking aloud, still aghast at having brought this down on Phelim.

Alexia did not seem to hear, intent as she was on watching the lighting of the Bush. As the fuel-soaked rags spurted into

140

tufts of flame high above Phelim's head, she shouted, *'RUN, PHEE!'*

Startled, drink-fuddled, top-heavy, off-balance, Phelim set off, staggered back two paces, then began to waddle down the street. There was no heat—the fire was all on the top of the bale—but there was a popping roar, and shadows leapt out in all directions. He knew he could not carry such a weight from end to end of the town, but he would show willing. And surely it *must* get lighter as he went. The pitchfork handle ground into his collar bone, but he passed the dairy and the photographic studio.

Burning straws began to lift and swirl off the bale, the fire creating its own vortex of wind. The noise above his head grew louder. He stumbled past the chandler's and the post office. The crowd—a pebbledash of fire-lit faces—screamed at him, contorted with eagerness. He was past the boarding house and the florist.

That was far enough, surely. He had shown willing. But some of the town had been blessed and some of it not. The butcher signalled for Phelim to keep going past his shop; in his hand was a meat axe. He began to chant: 'Fire or blood! Fire or blood!' and the people picked up the words, while the drummers picked up the beat. *'Fire or blood! Fire or blood!'* Mr Pringle's old magic had brought them to fever pitch: their shouts pelted Phelim like rotten fruit. But he got past the butcher's, past the opening to Sheep Street.

The bale was burning now with a violence Phelim could feel right though the fork. It was like a tree buffeted by a hurricane. He could no longer see out for the curtain of falling debris which rained down all around him. He began to lose his sense of direction and stray off the middle of the road. The crowd pushed him back, with brooms and hoes and the poles meant for opening their shop blinds.

If he was Green Jack, why was this so hard? thought

141

Phelim. Why did it not come easy to him, if he was really Jack o' the Green? The fire seemed every bit as heavy as the straw had been.

'He'll never make it,' said Alexia. 'That fool costume will catch . . . ' She broke off with a cry as another rag within the bale exploded into flame spewing burning straw over the upturned faces. Phelim stumbled on past the chemist's shop.

The heat was intense now. The shaft of the pitchfork was itself alight, and a blizzard of straw tumbled down the street on a current of hot, undulating air. *'Fire or blood! Fire or blood!'* The chanting was a childish sing-song, all common sense melted out of the mob by the heat from the Burning Bush. Mr Pringle stared, the reflection of the fire rolling around the thick lenses of his spectacles.

Alexia, finding Phelim's shirt still in her hand, wetted it with half a mug of beer left neglected on a garden wall, and slipped it on, to trap her loose, flammable hair inside the collar. Then she ran into the orange maelstrom of drifting straw.

Phelim had come to a halt outside the bank, and despite the prodding of a woman with a window pole, he could go no further. The updraft of air to feed the fire had sucked his lungs empty, and there was nothing but smoke to refill them. His eyes were tight shut and oozing tears.

Alexia snatched the pitchfork out of his fists, paused to catch her balance, then ran with it—past the tobacconist and the terraced houses. The wet shirt gave off white steam as she ran. The bale was disintegrating now: a poppy head shaking out its seeds of fire. Clumps of burning straw buffeted the house-fronts, burned themselves out on doorsteps, settled on the woman with the window pole: a blessing of fire, wisps of incandescent luck.

The mood of the crowd changed suddenly, as they realized the danger, and they fell back, banging into Phelim who, in

142

his charred green motley and no longer illuminated, was almost invisible. He heard a woman say, 'Somebody do something.'

There was total silence then, but for the roar of the fireball balanced above Alexia's head. Just below the metal ferrule of the fork-head, the pitchfork handle changed from wood to brittle ash, and the last thirty pounds of straw fell. When they did, the twin tines of the fork were plainly visible inside, glowing red, melting into a heart-shaped lump of shrapnel.

The metal struck her on the head, but she did not go down. Enveloped in fire, she remained standing, stationary, a black silhouette. As the shirt caught light, her hair was set loose to fly upwards—a stook, a sheaf of burning hair, haloing the shadow of a girl.

15

The Witch's Ladder

Suddenly there was no one about. The crowd melted away. The street lay three-in-the-morning quiet, the bonfires at either end shifting and settling as if deeply ill-at-ease. Only Mr Pringle stood anchored to the spot by the weight of responsibility. His rite of fire had come to nothing. It had also cost a life.

Phelim knelt down beside Alexia. It was difficult to see her on the dark ground, because every part of her was blackened by burning. Behind him, the Obby Oss swayed and keened and banged the rim of his round body against a lamp-post.

'Wuz my doing!' he wailed. 'Wuz all my doing! If I had not named you . . . '

'No,' said Phelim. 'No. It was the shirt. I gave her the shirt. It passed to her. I passed it.' He explained about the Washer-at-the-Ford, about the omen, while the Oss tossed and heaved around him like a boat without oars.

'It weren't your intent, zon. You meant her no harm.'

'But if I'd said. If I'd told her. If I hadn't kept it secret . . . '

'Then Fate would have worked its way out just the zame. What zay? If you han't kept secret. If I had. What then?' *Thud thud*, on and on he banged with his flank, partnering the lamp-post in a waltz of misery.

Phelim, as a frenzied afterthought, was trying to pull away the fragment of shirt, to undo what the shirt or the fire or Fate or all three had done to his friend, when from the dark, smoking heap on the ground came a sound.

'Alex? *Alexia? Can you hear me?'*

Mr Pringle, tucking his knees up high, ran for help, for first-aid, for a blanket, to find a doctor. But Phelim knew better than to go. Twice before he had run away from Alexia. He would not run away from her again. 'Alexia? You shouldn't have taken it off me. The fire. I could've done it. It should've been me. It should have.'

'I was your Maiden. I told you. "Alexia". For helping. Listen . . . '

Mr Pringle came back, noisy in his panic. 'Cover her over! Here! Look! Put this over her! I've sent for the doctor. He'll be right along . . . ' He made it impossible to hear what Alexia was saying; her words had no breath behind them: shape but no volume. Phelim put his face down close to hers, almost touching.

'Ladder . . . ' it sounded like. 'Witch's Ladder. Ask Sweeney . . . '

With a loud, flapping flurry, Pringle dropped a heavy greatcoat over Alexia. As it fell, it expelled from under it a flurry of dust and ashes, half-burned straws and Alexia's last words: ' . . . *Ask Sweeney.*'

The darkness congealed around them, so clagging thick that the dying bonfire had no power to dilute it. Out of this darkness, like the lees settling in a bowl, came a figure. The gait was bandy, splayed at the knee so that only the edges of his feet touched the ground. But as he came closer, Sweeney seemed to abandon his efforts to avoid contact with the ground and to walk normally. The ragged hem of his coat looped down and dragged along the ground. The spokes within his coat were all bunched and buckled. He looked like an angel who had been dropped into the tarpits of Hell and dragged himself halfway out again. The only sign that remained of Sweeney's Fear was the convulsive trembling that shook him from head to foot. He must have been watching from the rooftops.

'You came down,' said the Oss.

Sweeney shrugged so that his coat rattled. 'When the worst has happened, what is left to fear?'

Phelim was too mired in his own grief to see anything remarkable in Sweeney's descent to the ground. 'Where were you?' he growled, and Sweeney flinched as if he had been kicked. 'Where were you? Alexia's dead. She burned.'

'Not the first witch to burn,' said Sweeney.

Phelim threw a wild punch at him. It struck Sweeney in the collar bone, but he did not step back. Phelim hit him twice more, then began beating his fists against Sweeney's chest, as he had against his own locked front door when the glashans shut him out. Little tussocks of dust flew up. A fob watch lodged inside Sweeney's dusty military tunic slipped down at last and smashed on the road, spring and cog wheels spilling out. Phelim sank down on his knees and tried to sweep the pieces together with his fingertips, spring and cogwheels and circle of glass. 'I'm sorry. I'm sorry. I'm sorry. I'm sorry,' he said.

'Sanfairyanne, lad,' said Sweeney. *'Ça ne fait rien.'*

When Phelim began to cry, it was the Oss who told him harshly to stop. 'Shame on you, Green Man. Would you cry back the dead?'

'Cry back—?'

'Don't you know it's a wickedness? To cry back the dead?'

'You sound like my sister,' said Phelim bitterly. *'Turn off the taps, Baby McPhee.'*

Sweeney put a hand on Phelim's shoulder. 'It's an old notion. You have to make allowances. We hail from a world of old notions.'

'If crying would bring her back, I'd cry a sea-full.' He wiped his face on a handful of costume.

'So would we, son. So would we.'

The turning tide dropped a sudden mist of cold drizzle over the unlit houses of Storridge, doused the dying embers of the two bonfires. The twin stacks of part-burned timber settled again; some planks, a branch, a broken-runged ladder all slumped out beyond the ring of ash and smouldering debris.

The Witch's Ladder. Ask Sweeney. Ask Sweeney, the rain seemed to whisper on the slate roofs.

'Sweeney—what is the Witch's Ladder?'

Sweeney was scattering the mechanics of his watch with a bare foot. Seeing Mr Pringle's tutti-pole lying discarded in the street, he went and picked it up and began rending the bouquets of flowers off the broom handle, tossing them back towards the greatcoat and the body beneath it. 'Don't know, son.'

Phelim too began to strip the flower-heads off his costume. 'Yes you do. Alexia said. Ask Sweeney. The Witch's Ladder.'

Sweeney seemed genuinely bewildered, his face working with the effort of puzzling over the words. Perhaps in overcoming some of his Fear he had lost some of his Knowledge.

A distant dustbin rattled. Mr Pringle who, until then, they had thought gone, got up from among the greengrocer's bins and said, 'I have a book.' His face was as white as goat's cheese. He was struggling his arms out of his shirt-sleeves, trying to give Phelim something of his own, to compensate for what was lost.

The Obby Oss rushed at him, hooves flying, hide flapping. 'Hast thou not done evil enough?'

Mr Pringle fell back among the bins, rubbing his kicked shins, but he did not run away. 'I have a book,' he said again. 'There was something in it about . . . the Witch's Ladder, but I . . .'

Sweeney went rigid. He sprang up the lamp-post and clung

147

there for a moment, like a monkey on a stick, eyes monkey-wide.

   'Boney was a warrior,

   Way-hey-ah!

  Boney was a warrior, Jean Francois! . . . Take the boy away, Oss. Take him on to the Worm's Head. I'll come along after. Take him away! Go on, *go!'* And he flapped his coat so violently that the Oss's ribbons fluttered, Phelim's tears dried to salt on his face, and the dust rose up off the mound that was Alexia.

'Now that the shirt is gone, thou hast less cause to fear from the Worm, eh, boy?' said the Oss as they cantered out along the Stoor Head road.

'Now Alexia's gone I don't give a fig,' said Phelim. Grief had given way to a drab, dragging fatigue—an indifference to anything and anyone. Yes, he would fight the Worm. It was futile, but he would do it. Nothing else commended itself as a better way of spending the rest of his life. But he felt the same dull, leaden sense of worthlessness that he felt when his sister launched into one of her tirades against him: *'Lazy, grubby, good-for-nothing son of a tinker's donkey! Not worth the prunes on your plate, nor the stones when you've eaten them!'* Then and now, it was as if a sea-anchor were holding his heart to the seabed.

He did not want to leave Alexia's funeral in the hands of a madman. But there again what did it matter? Dead was dead. Her blood was flowing now down the Braide Brook, past the Washerwoman's Ford, and out to sea. Ultimately it would flow as far as Hy Brasil and clog their gutters and water their colourless flowers. The girl without a shadow was all shadow now. He could feel the chill of it all over him.

The Oss came to a sharp halt and leaned so far back that

Phelim slithered off. They were confronted by a cliff of such prodigious height that in the pre-dawn it was impossible to see as far as its summit. And it was smooth—shingled in overlapping tiles of glass-smooth rock.

The Stoor Worm's jaw lay part-submerged in the sea, part sunk into the soft rind of the earth by sheer dint of its weight. Sand and shingle and composted seaweed had piled up all around it. Distance had not shown up the head for what it was; now that they were close up they still saw no pulsing veins, no subterranean rush of blood, nothing zoological. The scales of its foreleg (and of the head resting on that foreleg) were platelets of rock. It was too large even to be frightening. Besides, it did not fit inside his head now, because his head was full of Alexia.

'We'll have to go round another way,' said Phelim. 'Up the slope of its back. Over the shoulder.'

But the Oss only pranced and sidled in and out of the sea, all colour gone from its ribbons. ' 'Twould take a week. More. And bring uz only to the ears and skull-top. And Hatchlings all the way. Here we are, and here it lieth. Best done now.'

Phelim scowled horribly. 'Oh well. Good a place as anywhere to fail, I suppose.' And he set about trying to climb.

From end to end of the cove he searched for a foothold, while the Oss fretted and kept watch for Hatchlings. But though Phelim reached up, climbed on boulders, piled up some old wooden pallets and an oil-drum, the rock was too smooth to climb. 'Stand close,' he told the Oss. 'I'll climb on your back.'

The Oss stood close, its disc-shaped body trembling like a clashed cymbal, and Phelim stood on his back. But though he reached up and felt about, he could still find no handhold. It was as if the cliff were made of glass.

'Use these,' said a familiar voice, and Sweeney was there, a shabby, unremarkable figure now. In place of his spoked coat he was wearing the greatcoat Mr Pringle had laid over Alexia. It was far too big for him, so that he appeared to have shrunk. He looked vulnerable, in his bare feet, confined to the ground, thrusting a hessian sack up at Phelim who stood balanced high above him.

'At least I have my Fool and my Horse now,' said Phelim.

'Maiden, too,' said Sweeney, jerking his head towards the sack. 'It came to me what she meant, and it made sense of all. There's a sense to all things. Just a matter of finding it. Use them then bring them back. Bring back every last one.' His voice was sad and soft and musical, no trace of raucous rhyme. Phelim, still standing on the Oss's back and leaning against the cliff, opened the sack and looked inside. There was not very much to its contents.

Only a few bones.

Phelim dropped the sack, and it rattled like spillikins. Alexia's skull rolled out like a giant ostrich egg, and came to rest on its back, empty eye sockets looking up at him.

Phelim leapt at Sweeney and the two of them went down in a heap, Phelim's fists flailing, his teeth clenched so hard that he ground his own words to pieces. 'You beast! You vile oaf! You . . . you . . . you . . . '

The Oss spun and reeled like a coracle.

'How could you! How could you?!' Kneeling across the old man, Phelim had his hands in the matted hair and was beating Sweeney's head on the ground. 'Her *bones*? You give me her *bones*?! *How* . . . ?'

The sickness which overtook Phelim was all that saved Sweeney from having his own skeleton stripped bare. The boy crawled away, not caring that his knees gouged into Sweeney's chest, that his shoes caught him a blow in the face—'You horrible, disgusting old madman'—then flopped flat along the ground.

The Obby Oss stood on Phelim's hair so that his face was

pinned to the ground. Phelim tried to push the skinny black fetlock away, but the Oss stood firm. Its soft, West Country voice burred in his ear. ''Tis the Witch's Ladder, zon. Girl knew it and Sweeney knew it. 'Tis the Witch's Ladder.'

'Get off me!'

'She were a witch, boy! Things fall out as they should. All a part of the same Magic, see?'

When Phelim opened his mouth to answer, it half filled with shingle. He wriggled and raged. 'Is that any reason she can't be decent buried?'

The Oss lifted a hoof and freed Phelim's hair. 'No lack of rezpect,' he murmured in a soft, clogged voice. 'Sweeney hath done no more, no less than wuz her wish.' His hoof nudged the sack with great delicacy towards Phelim who turned his face away. 'She wants to be of help, as her name framed her to be. Wilt thou thwart her? Out of *niceness*? Magic is not *nice*. Magics wuz never *nice*.'

Phelim curled himself into a tight ball and put his hands over his ears. *'Why don't you leave me alone? Why don't you both heave off out of here and leave me be? You brought me here. I never wanted to come, but you brought me anyway. Now why don't you just . . . '*

There was a scuffling of hooves, a clicking of shingle, and when Phelim opened his eyes again, they had taken him at his word and gone. All that remained were Sweeney's bare footprints in a patch of gritty sand, and the sack of bones which had once been his friend.

Prudence's insults came back so vividly that they might as well have been daubed on the glassy rock. *'Nothing but a sackful of trouble, that's you. Headache with a dirty face. What's your skull full of, I'd like to know! Potato peel and chicken droppings, that's what, Phee McRubbish.'*

He laid his hand on the sack and a kind of shiver went through him. But it was not fright. He no longer cared enough about himself to be afraid. While he had had Alexia for a friend, he had minded. 'Everybody's somebody,' she had said. But now she was gone what did it matter that he was supposed to defeat a monster the size of Anglesey and had no means to do it? He had come all this way, and he could not even climb up to confront the beast.

Phelim took out a long bone—a thigh bone, perhaps—and held it up to see if it cast a shadow. But the sky was overcast. He could not tell. Well, he could bury her, even if the others would not. He could put up a marker with her name on it, a proper marker which cast a proper shadow. Phelim looked around for something to dig with—could find only a shoulder-blade fallen from the sack.

Six inches down, the sea came up to meet him in the hole.

Frustrated past enduring, Phelim turned and hurled the scapula against the cliff. *'It's all your fault, Alexia! I told you I was nobody!'* It sank like a cleaver into snow.

Ashamed and appalled, he went to retrieve it, but it was wedged hard—a step projecting from the cliff. When he rested his weight on it, he felt a seismic thump, like distant quarrying. The Worm's pulse.

Gathering together all the bones, he separated large from small, leaving all the tiny, delicate ones, some as thin as needles, some as small as a gambler's dice, in a pile on the surface of a large flat rock. The large ones he put into the sack, the corner of which he knotted through a belt-loop of his trousers. Then he began to climb, driving rib after tibia after ulna into the hide of the Stoor Worm. He soon developed a systematic way of retrieving the bones below him to drive in higher up, above his head. Pitons of bone. At every step he expected the rungs of his ghoulish ladder to snap, but they held as true as iron, and penetrated the glassy slabs of rock as if it were balsa.

By the time he paused for breath and looked down, the cove

below was the size of a horseshoe, the sea a gunmetal carapace over the round back of the Earth. The town of Storridge showed as a canker on the flank of a geological ridge, a cluster of barnacles on a whale, a wart on the neck of the Stoor Worm.

It was all a matter of adjusting his perspective. He had not been thinking big enough. He had expected a dragon-shape such as a pair of hills sometimes suggest. But the Stoor Worm was not *in* the landscape; it *was* the landscape, though several thousand years of sleep had blurred its outline with topsoil, dunes, forest and ridged fields. He was climbing its shin—the thickness of a fore-leg—and on top of the leg rested the head. No rucking of the earth's skin, no collision of land masses, no wearing away by a million tides could account otherwise for the vast massif which bulged up into the sky and out into the sea.

Through the bone pitons, Phelim felt the heartbeat of the waking beast. Perhaps before the Great War it had beaten once a year, but as the guns roared on and the mortars thumped, its pace had quickened—to once a month, then once a week, then once a day. Now he felt the Worm's heartbeat three or four times an hour as he climbed. Steam rose, too, where the sea fret wetted the Worm's skin. Its temperature was rising, no question.

The sea fret dampened his palms; it made the bones harder still to hold. The sound of his own breathing seemed to come from somewhere outside him. Strange birds—some of them Hatchlings for all he knew—flew by and inspected him with beady black eyes.

Suddenly, without warning, a water-leaper, blind and stupid, jumped or fell from its hatching place high above and landed on Phelim's head, scrabbling for a moment amid his slippery hair before losing its grip and falling down inside the back of his borrowed shirt. As he ripped out his shirt tail with one hand, the water-leaper fell on down, though for a long time Phelim still clung to the bone rung, eyes shut, breathing so hard that his head spun, and hearing the sound of his own voice echoing: *'Get it off me!*

. . . off me!

. . . off me!'

The further he climbed, the more his muscles gibbered uncontrollably with fatigue. His hands and arms and calves were threaded with pain. What did he think he could do anyway, when he reached the Stoor Worm's head? But what could he do, other than go on climbing: he was too weary to go back down.

A ledge. Phelim felt it before he saw it, one hand sliding over the rim of red-veined rock. He pulled himself up on to a broad plain of rock, thinking he had reached the top. But of course he had not. A stone's throw ahead of him rose a wall of vertical white slabs pitted with caves and colonized by seabirds. There was a stench of fish, guano, and decay.

As he got to his feet, a hundred guillemots rose in panic and swooped by, uttering their swearing screams, rattling their wings, so that he stumbled backwards almost to the brink. He had reached the lip of the Stoor Worm and was looking at its teeth, the rotting teeth of a sleeping monster. Cavities as large as Norman windows allowed him to see beyond the teeth into the cathedral cavern of the mouth, though at first his eyes, sore and daylight-dazzled, could see only darkness. Instead, he *heard* the contents of the cave: a noise like frozen lakes cracking under the strain of spring; like glaciers creeping, like icebergs fracturing.

As Phelim's eyes grew accustomed to the gloom of the Stoor Worm's mouth, he saw the seventy-score eggs incubating on the warmth of her tongue. Stones and boulders and pebbles lay about as haphazardly as rubble, stones which the Stoor Worm had clenched in her jaws as she lapsed into unconsciousness.

154

Some stones, awash in their mother's bitter saliva, had already hatched. The broken halves lay jagged-edged in the brackish pools. The rest would follow soon enough, hatching into the stuff of nightmares.

With a noise like a pistol shot, the boulder beside Phelim split, and its two halves rolled apart, so that he had to jump aside or be crushed. There, hooded in slimy albumen, a pantheon, fumbling blindly for life, flung out a paw which curled around Phelim's knee.

16

A Dream of Falling

Phelim intercepted the paw with his hand and held it. The claws within its velvety feet were still soft. Enfeebled by the effort of hatching, it rested for a moment, globules of albumen slithering off its starry pelt, a panther but leopard-spotted with constellations of gold. It was beautiful. When he dropped the sacking over its blind, kitten's eyes, it ceased to move, like a parrot falling silent in the dark. It neither withdrew its paw, nor groped any further for the light.

Easing himself free, Phelim picked up two stones, as big as his hands could hold, and ran with them to the edge of the cliff, flinging them out into empty space to shatter far below. Then he went back to the hatching rock and rolled the pantheon, too, to its destruction. He began to fill the sack with the stones he could lift. Some were warm. Some were clicking.

When he came to lift the sack, it was far too heavy, of course. He had to drag it fifty yards to the cliff edge before throwing the stones over one by one. Even as he did it, he knew he could not win. Some of the boulders were far bigger than he was, some as big as haystacks. Even those as big as his head he could not lift. On the second trip to the cliff edge, the fabric of the sack tore, and the stones inside spilled out again, rolling and chinking together. And there were so many! He could run to and fro till his aching backbone crumbled: the Stoor Worm was brooding thousands of Hatchlings in her sleeping mouth.

Besides, he was repelled by what he was doing.

Standing on the very brink of the Worm's lip, the exquisite

smoothness of the pebble in his hand made him look at it afresh—at its mottled whiteness. One silent minim. An egg. Suddenly, he did not want to pit himself against the Worm. Evil or not, he felt no animosity towards her. In fighting her, he could only become what she was: malevolent, destructive. How was this raiding of nests any better than Sweeney plucking songbirds out of the air and prising open their chests. And Sweeney had good cause.

Phelim thought of Assipattle slicing and slashing with his sword, and it was not the preposterousness of the myth that struck him (one man fighting this sub-continent of a beast) as the violence, the kill-or-be-killed pettishness of it all. How could you be angry with an earth tremor for shaking down your house? How could you be angry with a monster for existing, or a sleeper for waking up? All his life his sister had hated Phelim with a seething resentment—not for anything he did (he could see that now) but simply because he repelled her. He was the Stoor Worm in her landscape. The thought inspired a certain *sympathy* between Phelim and the Worm in whose mouth he stood. How can you hate a geological feature?

He walked among the uneven, snaggled teeth and watched a boobrie—billed, web-footed, absurd as a duck but larger than a bull—hatch and drag itself away into the gullet at the back of the mouth. Presumably each Hatchling crawled or flew or crept down the monster's cavernous alimentary canal, through gently sloping miles of winding gut, to the creature's vent and out into the world that way. Only a few could climb sucker-footed down the precipitous cliff, or survive a fall from her lip. Would Phelim also have to go down that way? He was perfectly sure he was too tired to climb back down the way he had come. Presumably the whole bulk of the great sleeper's body teemed with Hatchlings right now.

He mistook the glint for the shine of animal eyes watching

157

him. But it was simply the Faeries' Golconda, their treasure hoard. Just as they had said, it lay in the Worm's keeping, piled up under her prodigious tongue. The gold, for the most part, was not in coin but in strange, asteroidal lumps of pure soft ore. Quartz and onyx and pyrite were as plentiful as platinum and emeralds, for the Faeries' values were not the same as men's. They hoarded as magpies hoard—for prettiness. Globules of mercury welled in glittering teardrops from bone-white millet shells and the papery seedpods of honesty. Puddles of petrol shot through with rainbow were as lovely to the Faeries as rubies or diamonds.

Phelim stood for a long while staring at the great mound of treasure and trash, thinking of Murdo and of the sapphire sea which had claimed him. At last he bent and picked up a handful of gold and just one gemstone, slipping them into his tight trouser pocket where they pressed against his groin as the florins had done. He was not sure why he did it. It was not as if he expected to outlive the day.

'Sing you back to sleep, shall I?' he called out derisively, but his voice came out so loud, and echoed so gigantically around the cathedral-sized cavern that he clapped his hand over his mouth, half expecting the Worm to wake there and then. Phelim willed the sound away, suppressing the echoes with little downward pats of his hands. Silence.

It was then that he saw it. It was moving not towards the gullet, but roaming in among the stones and boulders and pebbles which were the Worm's brood. He knew at once that it was not a Hatchling. Perhaps he had brought with him the Knowledge of Sweeney.

He knew at once that it was not a mouse, for all it was mouse-like. It resembled a mouse, just as the Oss resembled a horse. Its fur was long and pale, and its outline blurred, out of focus, so that Phelim automatically blinked, for a clearer view. It was the size of a rat and its movements were slurred, as if under water. There was a luminosity about its greyness, too, which put Phelim in mind of the merrows' fish pots, the glimmering souls trapped inside.

Alexia's words came back to him, as though she were speaking in his ear. 'I saw the soul-mouse come from your mouth.' Phelim held perfectly still. Maid and Horse and Madman had given him the wisdom to know that here was the soul-mouse of the Worm.

The Stoor Worm was dreaming. Somewhere high above, beneath lids of leaf-mould and roots, its eyeballs flickered, shaking pebbles loose, disturbing birds from their branches. The Stoor Worm was dreaming. Here was its soul, making an excursion out of deep sleep into the dream-filled hinterland of shallow dozing.

That such a beast should have so small a soul! Why, the hessian rag of sack which Phelim held in his hand was large enough to smother the glowing grey creature. If he could just hold still . . .

He told himself that his blood was sap, that his limbs were clay, that his hair was moss. He held so still that faintness roared in his ears and nausea swelled into the bole of his stomach. The soul-mouse, whiffling and pottering around the broken shards of hatched stones, looked directly at him, with eyes the colour of burning peat. And the Stoor Worm dreamed of a Green Man.

Right over his foot the soul-mouse crept. Like the flickering newsreels from France, its movements were disjointed, colourless, silent, horrific. Like the faces in the newsreels, it looked up at Phelim without seeing him and moved on, out between the decaying teeth, on to the sunlit plateau of the Worm's lip. Phelim had so long refrained from blinking that his eyes were dry as pebbles.

Now he extended an arm, dropped the sacking over the mouse, fell on it, clutched the whole parcel to his chest, and rolled on top of it with all his weight. He slammed it against the ground, picked up a stone and smashed it down on the hessian.

'That's for her! That's for her! That's for Alexia!'

Spittle burst between his teeth as he shouted the name. Inside the hessian it was not a mouse he was killing but Mr Pringle: his pebble lenses, his pigeon chest, his colourless hands, his well meaning smile.

'Die! Die! Die! Die! Die!'

He bit into the parcel with his teeth, pummelled it with both fists. Noises came out of him that were neither words nor even human: barks and yelps and screams and grunts. Then he picked up the soul-mouse and ran with it to the edge of the precipice. With an effort so large that it almost carried him over as well, he threw the Stoor Worm's soul out into thin air.

And the Worm dreamed of pain, of falling and of pain—of sea for a sky and the sky for a sea, and spiralling images of her own form couched sphinx-like between sea and land. She dreamed of falling, of cold, of the airless world of her children the merrows. She dreamed the taste of salt and the lightness of buoyancy, of the swaying swash of deep-water currents, of sub-marine islands and trenches of dark.

From under the ground, from far beyond the palisade of teeth or the stalactite gullet came a rumbling groan, a thunder, a roar, a death rattle which shed topsoil in tons off the Worm's spine. The noise hit Phelim where he stood, hands over ears. He felt the noise go through him like sand through a riddle. It jarred all the soft organs of his body, jumbled up his heartbeat, made his nose bleed. When it finished he did not know whether the silence was real or a symptom of deafness. He had the impression that his eyes were bleeding, too, but found that the wetness crawling down his cheeks was only tears.

Phelim shuddered violently. He had not known he was

160

going to kill the mouse. He had not known he was capable of killing anything. Though the Stoor Worm was dead, he felt no conquering triumphs, only an unspeakable sorrow—as if his chest had been torn open and his heart ripped out. He was one of Sweeney's birds.

Deep within the gut of the dead Worm, a score of Hatchlings felt their mother's anguish, felt the pipes and chambers of her body begin to cool. In her death throes, some of them were squeezed on their way towards the vent, others were regurgitated into the gullet, into the mouth. Dogs and brags, ushteys and coranieids, calygreyhounds, bagwyns and griffins came crowding towards Phelim amid a stench of bile. He tried to dodge past them, but they formed a solid wall, evil made flesh.

He stepped back, but the Worm's mouth, slackening in death, sagged away from the teeth, and the ground under his feet was no longer level. He lost his balance and stumbled backwards, one pace, two paces, out into the same nothingness that had swallowed up the soul-mouse.

17

Aisling

There was nothing to grab but the Witch's Ladder. The Hatchlings fleeing their mother's mouth stumbled blindly over the edge, as well, and fell on his head like an avalanche. A dozen different shrieking squeals, a dozen kinds of stench jarred his brain to a standstill. He thought to be swept away by them, but he clung on and clung on, first by one hand, then by two, then finding, by fumbling with his feet, a firm foothold on the lowest of the rungs. Alexia's bones had slid into the hide as easily as hooks into a fish's jaw, and they held just as fast. And yet when he lifted one end, the bone slid out again like an oar from water.

'Bring them back,' Sweeney had said. 'Bring back every last one.' Perhaps, after all, he meant Alexia to have a decent burial.

Without the sack, it was harder than hard. He pushed the rungs inside his shirt, his borrowed shirt: Alexia's bones lay hard up against his ribs. It felt as if his own skeleton had come unthreaded and was rattling about inside his clothing. The smell of ash and dead fires enveloped him as he bent and twisted and leaned down to plant rungs low and lower for the never-ending descent. Soon his calves and forearms were so threaded with cramp that he had to prise open his own fingers one at a time from each rung. In crouching down, knees splayed to drive yet another bone into the cliff face, the ones within his shirt slipped out between the buttons, and fell . . . right into the outstretched hands of Mad Sweeney, thirty feet below.

Sweeney and the Oss had dodged the falling Hatchlings and buried them hurriedly under mounds of shingle. Now the

162

incoming waves withdrew from these shingle barrows with distaste, lips curled.

'Every last one, boy. Every last one. Don't scant for one.'

All of the tiny bones already lay in the base of the cauldron— the little metatarsals of the foot, the vertebrae like empty cotton reels, the catapult-shaped collar bones, the patellae like the white caps of mushrooms. It was not the kind of cauldron Phelim associated with magic—just an old oil drum washed up bent and buckled on to the beach. And he should never have looked inside. The skull looked back at him like someone screaming, drowning. He wanted to plunge his hands into the cauldron and pull it to the surface, but the seawater was already too hot.

They had lit the fire from flotsam and jetsam, rope ends and netting. There was a chance the tide would rise too high and put out the fire beneath the cauldron: they should have waited until they were off the beach. But Sweeney could not wait. He ran to and fro, feeding the flames with seagull feathers and empty cigarette packets he found on the foreshore. The water came to the boil, setting the bones moving in a macabre dance.

'I cannot look. I cannot stay!' cried the Oss, and galloped away along the beach. They could see him running at the waves as if they were female, then fleeing as they rushed at him with their larger, more potent magic.

'I found something,' said Phelim casually. 'While I was up there, I found something odd.'

Sweeney continued to scour about for feathers to fuel the fire, eyeing the sea, fearing the worst.

'It was a nest—last spring's. No eggs. Just a dead bird.'

Sweeney was hunkered down now, trying to blow more life into the fire, his face red from the heat and the blowing.

'A swallow, I think it was,' said Phelim as casually as if he were just making conversation. 'Hard to tell. It was all falling apart.'

Sweeney's hand hesitated, came to a halt. His eyes flicked in Phelim's direction. 'A swallow?'

'I think so. And do you know what? It had this sort of shine inside it. This odd shine. So I looked closer, and there it was!'

Sweeney breathed in such a faceful of smoke that he began to cough and splutter and his eyes ran. He looked at the sea, at Phelim, at the steam rising from the cauldron. It was as if there were one too many worries to contend with. 'What? What? What? What? What?' He sounded like a broody old chicken laying an egg.

'A gem. A jewel. Don't know what kind. What do I know about jewels? Pretty, though. I suppose the bird picked it up for prettiness—like a magpie. Swallowed it by accident. Do you think? You wouldn't think the gullet would be big enough.'

Sweeney's face was turned upwards now, flat-on to the sky, as he gazed up the glassy cliff, all means gone of climbing it. Phelim allowed himself a smile. 'So I brought it down. I thought you might like it. You know. A souvenir.'

Sliding his fingers into his tight little pocket, he held out the ruby to Sweeney who came for it with both hands cupped, his mouth agape with wonder, speechless. Phelim smiled cheerfully, knowing that the smile would hide the lie.

Sweeney's milky blue eyes searched every inch of Phelim's face for a sign of a trick, of a practical joke at his expense. His thoughts were so plain they were almost audible. He had never told Phelim about his search, so how could the boy be making it up?

'You truly found it? In a swallow? No word of a lie?'

Phelim looked Sweeney directly in the eye. 'Honest. Inside its chest.'

Sweeney stretched out a hand and held it, fingers spread, on Phelim's face, as if he were touching wood or a talisman. His other fist clenched tight round the gemstone. 'Forgive me, boy. Naturally. Ever-Good Green. There's no guile in you. Nothing in you but the truth.'

Phelim's smile did not so much as falter.

Suddenly the old man's entire bearing changed. He seemed to grow taller, so that his coat no longer swamped him. His head lifted. The squinnying creases around his eyes relaxed. His teeth no longer clenched edge-to-edge, settled into a natural bite, so that his jawline softened. His face resolved itself into a peace, as if at long last the deafening sound of gunfire had ceased to hammer in his ears.

'Ask me for no more knowledge, boy,' he said, in a soft, deep voice. 'My Fear has left me.'

In the next instant, an exceptionally large wave broke and the sea swirled in, swilling around and under the cauldron. With it, all Phelim's fear returned.

The fire was extinguished, and half of its fuel dragged back down the beach by the receding water. The hot base of the cauldron crawled with white steam. The noise of bubbling fell silent.

Sweeney restrained Phelim from running to look inside. 'Come away, boy,' he said, as if failed magic was a sight best not seen.

Then the Oss came galumphing back, hysterical, overwrought, like a child who has eaten too much sugar. 'What's done? What's done? What's come to pass?'

Sweeney kept tight hold of Phelim's sleeve. 'The boy has restored my wits,' he said solemnly, and the Oss gave a sharp hinny which might have been joy and might have been derision, then raced off again along the beach.

'There's a great lot of Hatchlings already about,' said Phelim. 'Do you think they have to be . . . I mean, must I . . . '

165

'You have done sufficient. More than sufficient,' said Sweeney. 'They will wreak their havoc, but the world will explain them away. It has an art these days for explaining away its magics. Do you not agree? Its nightmares.'

Phelim saw it was true. The Great War had devoured millions of men, mislaying them under slurrying mud. And yet already people were pretending it had not happened, glad to put it out of mind, trying not to think about it. They could easily ignore a few corn wives on their fields, a few boobries among the cows.

'Storridge Town will never be the same,' said Phelim. 'Not after what happened.'

'Don't you believe it, Green Man. They will forget sooner than all the rest. Just as soon as they can, like drinkers waking up with a headache, knowing the night before would shame them if they could remember it. I tell you, by now Storridge Town will be all teacups and parson pi, and no one looking another in the eye.'

'But deep down they'll never forget how they killed Alexia . . .'

'No.'

They both turned, and there she stood, in the oil barrel, scruffy as a cat emerging from a dustbin.

It was and it was not her. In place of her dandelion white hair was a flame-red frizz. Her face, which had been uniformly white before, like snow, looked as though the snow had begun to melt into hollows. Hollows in her eyes, under her cheekbones, in the angle of her collarbones. It takes shadows to make a face beautiful.

Steam from the cooling water wreathed around her, as smoke had done the night before, and her hands were still upraised. The left hand wanted for a finger.

They did not dash towards her, or shout her name, but stood gaping stupidly. Even Sweeney had not fully believed in the ancient story of the Witch's Ladder.

166

Phelim took one step closer. 'Are you a ghost?' he asked.

She held her flame-red head on one side. 'No. No,' she said, as if considering this. 'Feel.'

He ought to have taken her outstretched hand, ought to have helped her out of the oil drum, but he could see that she was naked and did not dare go close. Instead he said, holding off at a distance, 'You have your shadow back, look. Where have you been?' He was thinking of Braide Brook, of Hy Brasil, of the Devil.

The red-haired girl stifled a yawn. 'I dreamed a lot,' she said sleepily. 'I dreamt I was a ship—the keel . . . the ribs . . . ' She looked at her wrist, turning her arm this way and that. 'The sea was rough. It strained . . . It was a long voyage.' Suddenly she began to shiver.

Sweeney came to his senses and ran and swung his coat around her, revealing for the first time his small wiry frame, the braces holding up his ragged army breeches. He helped her to climb out of the oil drum, but it overturned and emptied its contents into the shingle around their feet.

'Did he do it? Or is it still to be done?' she asked in her sleepy voice.

Sweeney could barely contain his happiness. 'He did it! He did! While the Worm was dreaming. He killed its soul-mouse! He climbed up and he climbed down. He brought me back my wits, do you know? He brought me a ruby from out of a swallow!'

'I thought I dreamed of Assipattle,' said the girl, nodding, looking at Phelim with gratification. Taking the measure of him afresh. 'But of course it was him.'

'Us,' said Phelim decidedly. 'Maiden and Fool and Horse . . . '

Along came the Oss, squeezing air through his body like an accordion, to produce a blare of chords. 'And Jack o' Green!' he cried, with a chord in C major.

This time Phelim did not contradict him. All along he had

told them: not Jack Green, but Phelim Green. Now he did not quibble.

Phelim sat opposite Alexia in the cafeteria in Storridge. The afternoon light was low, and he tangled his hands together to cast the likeness of a dog on the wall beside hers; beside the shadow-dog she herself was making. 'You should change your name,' said the one dog to the other. 'No more "helping".'

'What will be the point of me, then?' asked the smaller of the two shadow dogs.

'That depends what you choose for a name.'

She looked across at him, struggling a little to dispel the dreamy smoke which hung all the time around her thoughts. 'What, though? I can't think.'

'You can have mine if you want. Doesn't suit me any more. The old one, I mean. "Phelim".'

Alexia was genuinely startled. 'Why, because you conquered the Worm? Are you going to be Jack o' Green now, because you killed the Worm?'

Phelim let out a laugh worthy of the Obby Oss. The manageress of the cafeteria pursed her thin lips and looked across, scowling disapproval. But she did not recognize the red-haired girl in the floral dress, nor the boy in long trousers and a clean, new shirt and jacket. Even if she had not tidied out of her mind that ghastly, tragic evening, she would not have recognized the witch or the Green Man.

'So I was lucky! Or whatever,' said Phelim, snarling with self-disgust. 'You weren't there. Whatever else I was, I wasn't "ever-good". I can prove it! I lied to Sweeney.'

'Is everything satisfactory?' asked the manageress, leaning between them to straighten the flowers disarranged in their vase by Phelim slapping the table.

'More cream buns,' said Phelim with a terseness worthy of

168

his sister. Then leaning across the table, he pushed his face as close to Alexia as if every other customer in the pink-and-white room was a coranieid listening. 'I did. I lied! I told him I found the jewel in a swallow, and I didn't. I lied. Yes. That's right. Does that sound like "ever-good" to you? And if I'm *not* Ever-Good, then I'm not magic either, and now Sweeney won't go on looking, and maybe he'll never really get back his wits. "Liar, liar, catch on fire": that's what my sister would say.'

'Ah yes. Your sister.' Apart from flinching slightly at the mention of burning, Alexia was less appalled than he had expected. 'Why?'

'Why what?'

'Why did you lie to Sweeney?'

Phelim fiddled with his cake fork, prodding the tablecloth into little ridges. 'I suppose because he wanted it so much. Because otherwise he was going to go on hating himself and thinking he was a coward. He might've spent another hundred years looking.'

'And now, instead, he will be happy. Yes?' said Alexia with the mildest of shrugs. 'Well, then.'

'Well then, what?'

'Well, then you did it out of kindness. Out of the "goodness of your heart", as they say. Kindness is goodness.' She covered his fork with her hand. 'Phelim, you killed the Stoor Worm. Of *course* you're magic. Of *course* you're good.'

He did not argue any more, though arguments rushed up into his head like Hatchlings into the mouth of their mother. Alexia did not know. Alexia had not seen his murderous savagery in killing the poor, soft, grey soul-mouse. She had not seen what a hugger-mugger fluke the whole thing had been. He knew he could not find the words to describe the shameful episode acted out on the Worm's lip. Instead he said, struggling with shyness, 'If the Devil can only see the blackness in a person, I'm surprised he saw you at all, Aisling.'

Again she started. 'Aisling? Is that my new name, then? I like it. What does it mean?'

Phelim half stood up, then sat down again. He looked in the shiny, silver teapot, not this time for her reflection but for his own. His freckle-splattered face bowed out at him, big-nosed, forehead stretched to an improbable bigness, as if crammed with knowledge. 'Dreamer. It means "dreamer",' he said uneasily. Why had he said that? How had he known? 'I must have heard it somewhere.'

Aisling leaned forward across the table, her wiry red hair brushing his face. 'From your father, maybe. What about your father? Tell.'

'No. No. I can't.'

'I told you my story.'

'I don't mean I won't. I mean I can't. I don't remember. I don't know. I was too young. We don't talk about him. Prudence says . . . My sister says . . . ' His face flushed a brilliant red. 'He was a waster. He was useless and lazy and ignorant and . . . '

'Says she.'

'And some day, if I don't shape up . . . some day, when the moon's full, they'll come for me like they did for him and take me away to . . . '

'Your account, sir,' said the manageress, and instead of more cream buns, set down a pink enamel saucer containing a slip of paper. She stepped back sharply from the face which looked up at her, not only because of the bright intensity of the eyes, but because it reminded her of the night the town lost its senses and broke adrift from civilization.

Phelim slipped a Georgian sovereign and a Spanish doubloon into the pink saucer and covered them quickly with the bill. They came from the Faeries' Golconda, so he was anxious now to leave.

170

'Does it ever occur to you, Phee,' said Aisling, checking her hair in the mirror on the wall. 'Does it ever occur to you that your sister might be the one who's in the wrong?'

18

Jack Green

'Where will you go?' Phelim asked Sweeney. 'You can't go back to Sweeney's Wood—except as a woodsman, I suppose.' He liked the sound of 'woodsman'. It recalled Little Red Riding Hood being rescued from the Big Bad Wolf, a task which would suit the new Sweeney admirably.

'How, a woodsman? No, by God! And cut down trees?' Sweeney looked as if Phelim had suggested he take to a life of crime. 'Nay. I thought I might take to a life of crime,' he said, 'and be revenged on the world's generals and sergeants by stealing of their snuff boxes.'

'How shalt thee get cloze up?' asked the Obby Oss, being both curious and practical.

'At military tattoos and polo matches,' said Sweeney without a moment's reflection.

Neither Phelim nor Aisling thought it a kindness to mention the passing of snuff boxes, the unfashionable nature of military tattoos. Both rather hoped Sweeney would be discouraged from his chosen career when he found there were none in the modern world.

'And then to the land,' Sweeney went on, stretching his arms wide as if to encompass the county. 'I shall work the land!'

The trees on the skyline held up bare branches as intricate as the veins in an eye, watching. The leaves of autumn lay in drifts at their feet. The Oss capered in and out of them, kicking up plumes of red and yellow and brown as high as his no-head.

'Little boy Green come blow up thy horn,
Thy maid's in the meadow

Babes yet to be born.

Where is the boy who baffled the Worm?

The time is a wasting and year's on the turn.'

Phelim laid a hand on the see-sawing, hee-hawing Oss who was singing the words that Sweeney ought to have sung: Oss, who had changed least of all and found no need to change. Soon he would gallop back to whatever supernatural meadow he grazed between May-days, one of the last survivors of the Old World, still loved, still prized, still welcome. The hide under Phelim's palm flickered, and the Oss barged against him in a clumsy gesture of affection.

'And you, Aisling. Where will you go?' Phelim asked, unable even to look at the girl with the flame-red hair. He was only asking so as to delay the awful moment when he would have to part company from his Maid and Fool and Horse, and cycle home.

'With you, of course,' said Aisling in her slow, drowsy voice.

They raced each other from the Braide Brook, riding their new bicycles as hard as they dared. Phelim was so intent on speed, so excited by the wind in his face that he did not realize when Aisling's chain came adrift and she had to stop, get off and wheel the bike. Arriving home, he was surprised to find she was not close behind him. He kicked open the rotting garden gate.

The garden lay just as he had left it, except that the flowers in the broken pots had withered away, and foxes had dragged off the dead chickens. Indoors, the stove was back in place against the wall, and there were no glashans sitting gnawing potatoes on the kitchen floor. A new regiment of lead soldiers marched across the kitchen table, each standing in a puddle of paint. He picked up one and examined it: the workmanship was sloppy. He put back the lid on a tin of enamel paint which was drying out.

'And just where have you been, Phee McFilth? Came back, did you? More's the pity!'

His sister came down the stairs like the pendulum of a clock, swaying from side to side to swing her stumpy legs down the steps, banging wall and banister in her eagerness to be at him. Despite all his resolve, all the changes which had overtaken him, Phelim felt the old helplessness come slurrying down on him, pinning him to the spot, pressing his shoulders into a stoop, oppressing his heart into speechlessness. 'Run off with the gypsies, did you? What have you got to say for yourself? Cat got your tongue? Ever give a moment's thought to me, did you? Ever think how I'd feel? Eh? Coming back to an empty house. Door wide open. Mayhem. Things stolen . . . '

'Did you see . . . anybody?' he felt driven to ask.

'Why? You been inviting friends in? You been making free with *my home*, Phee McHooligan? Tell you what I found. I found no food in the house, 'cepting a few mouldy buns. Found my window boxes ripped out. Found dirt trod into the kitchen floor . . . No word! Oh no, not so much as a note! Gone for weeks on end . . . '

She came bellying towards him and pushed her stomach hard up against him. He could see that she was thinner than before: no one to cook her meals or fetch home the shopping. There was a rim of grime inside the collar of her crumpled dress: no one to do her washing or ironing. Guilt and pity stirred in Phelim.

'I'm sorry if I worried you.'

'Worried? *Worried?*' Prudence's voice soared so high that it broke. 'You're nothing but a worry to me, Phee Green! Good mind to set the police on you for the shame and the nuisance of it. Where's my sevenpence, eh, you little thief! All spent, I suppose, on floozies and long trousers!'

Phelim's hand went at once to his pocket. His fingers ran through dubloons, crowns, and little asteroids of gold ore. Crumbs of hot cross bun scratched his fingertips. 'My father . . . ' he began tentatively, leaving his hand in his pocket.

Prudence gave a convulsive shudder. 'Make some dinner. Don't know how you managed to break it, but the stove won't light. After supper we'll discuss how you can make it up to me for running off. Just hope you've done nothing to shame me. I'm too upset now. Going to lie down . . . But don't you go thinking you've heard the last. Thought I was rid of you. Going to have to pull your weight if you want to stay under my roof, I can tell you! Another trick like this and you can pack your bags. You can! Don't think I don't mean it!' She began to stump up the stairs again, swaying even more wildly to raise her feet from stair to stair.

'Like my father?' said Phelim doggedly. 'He left, didn't he?'

'Good riddance to bad rubbish!' Her chubby face was jerked by a grimace as strong as the current which drags water down a plughole. 'Is that where you've been? Looking for your feckless father? Ferret. Stoat. Drunkard. Lunatic.' She looked suddenly like a witch herself, reciting an incantation. 'A shame and an embarrassment, that's what he was.'

Phelim spoke softly, trying not to provoke his sister. 'What did he do that was mad?'

Prudence clenched her two hands into a single fist which she jabbed at him as she talked. 'What did he *do* at all, I'd like to know?' she asked with a hysterical, swooping laugh. 'Tell lies. Read books. Go tramping about in the fields. Try and fill your head with lies all day and all night.'

'Lies?'

She leaned over the banister to blare at him. 'Lies, yes! Stories! Tales! Songs! Poems! Rubbish. Stories. Lies!' The banister rails rocked in their sockets. 'Forever *dreaming*. Used to talk to himself. Is that mad enough for you? Well? Used to say there was a man behind the stove—goblins or some such working in the fields. That's what drink does to a man. You take heed by it. Had nightmares, too. Woke the whole house with them.'

'What did he dream?'

'Dream? How do I know what he dreamt? What do mad people dream? Mother, she laughed it off. Not me. The day Mother died, I decided. Enough is enough. I told him: go and enlist. There's a war, I said. Haven't you heard? Kitchener needs you. Go and fight for your country, for God's sake.'

Phelim felt again the thud of the Worm's heartbeat through the soles of his feet, his own pulse too sluggish to push the blood through his brain. 'You sent our dad to the War?'

'Huh! Wouldn't go. Wouldn't sign up, cringing coward. Hun-lover. Told him: "you're a Hun-lover, you". Served him up white feathers to eat every mealtime. Painted a yellow stripe down the back of his shirt. Wasn't man enough, was he?' Prudence, who had never spoken of her father since the day of his departure, could not stop now that she had started. The bile streamed out of her like pus from a wound. 'So I had him committed.'

'Committed? To the Army?'

'Don't show your ignorance, Phee McStupid. To the asylum, of course. For the insane. Well, he *was* insane, wasn't he? Seeing things. Talking to people who weren't there. That's why we don't talk about him. That's why, if people ask, we just say he died. Is that nicely understood?'

Phelim sat down on a chair, his legs shaking too much to hold him. Prudence turned to continue her climb, telling him to cook some dinner for them both.

'Am I like him at all?' he called after her, but she did not hear. He knew the answer, of course. That was the reason Prudence hated him: because he so much resembled his father.

He relit the stove—it gave him no problems—and put down a saucer of milk beside it. Dragging out the sack of potatoes, he found it had been replenished from the fields: not by Prudence, of that he was sure. Peeling a panful, he put them on to boil, found a can of corned beef and a can-opener. Then he opened the door, plucked a vaseful of michaelmas daisies, and stood waiting for Aisling to come into view. A whole half hour passed. The potatoes cooked.

'You're making a draught,' Prudence complained coming downstairs to eat. 'Who's that coming? Get rid of her. Do let's keep ourselves to ourselves. I suppose you know my pony's wind has gone? Have something to do with that, did you? Had to shoot it: couldn't be ridden and there's no point in wasting feed. And the chickens! The chickens! Don't think you won't be paying for that, Phee McVandal. Don't think I won't make you pay.' She said it with relish, as if the favours he owed her would now be endless. 'I leave you alone for a day or two, and what happens? My bicycle in pieces, my animals are killed. When I find out what mischief you got up to . . . '

He could see that Prudence was working herself up to another tirade: a list of grievances to justify the lifelong war she had waged against Phelim and his father before him.

'I have another one coming,' said Phelim. 'Another horse.'

Prudence gave a snort which rattled her sinuses, and looked around with exaggerated puzzlement, her mouth crammed with potato. There was nothing to be seen but the girl wheeling her bicycle along the lane. No sign of a horse. 'Oh yes? Oh yes?' she said nasally. 'Been learning from your father, have you, Phee McLiar?'

If Phelim had been undecided before, he made up his mind then. Stepping to the door, plucking a blade of grass from the unmown lawn, he pinned it between the sides of his thumbs and blew—a loud, quacking blart. Such a vulgar noise. He could see Prudence thinking it: such a vulgar noise.

He blew again—a shriller note, this time. The red-haired girl pushing the bicycle stopped and looked back, moving aside as a great white horse came thudding out of the distance.

Not for a moment had Phelim doubted that it would come. He was his father's son, and Jack o' Green could have summoned an ushtey any day of the year. Jumping the garden wall, the creature did not stop its plunging gallop until it stood with its head overarching Phelim, its nostrils blowing in his face. Its backward hooves were hidden by the long grass of the lawn.

Prudence, after her initial shock, stared in admiration at this perfect piece of horseflesh, its luxuriant mane, its cascading tail, its sea-coloured eyes.

'Shall I fetch your saddle from the shed?' asked Phelim.

His sister giggled girlishly. 'Oh, I couldn't. Not any more. Not till I've lost a few pounds.' But Phelim was already fetching the saddle, and his foot was dragging the chicken coop over, to serve as a mounting block.

'Phelim!' called Aisling from the road. 'Phelim?'

The chicken coop creaked under Prudence's weight. The saddle was pulled off-centre as she wedged her fat foot into the stirrup and hopped.

'Where is my dad now?' asked Phelim, his hand on her rump, pushing her aboard. 'Is he still at the asylum?'

'Must be, I suppose. Unless he died. Best thing. No use to man nor beast, a madman. Now stand away, will you? Out of the way! Leave go!'

He did.

Foam from the ushtey's mouth spattered him as it jerked its head towards the lane. Sinking back on its haunches it took the wall in a standing leap, and was away down the road, fetching the leaves off the trees, the dust off the roadway, the dry ruins of old birds' nests out of the hedges. Prudence's shouting voice diminished until, like faery music, it was audible only in the imagination.

Phelim's hatred and anger went with it, sucked out of him like the nests out of the hedgerow. He was left with the same kind of emptiness as after killing the Worm. Aisling leaned her bike against the wall. She came within the gate, but stood a way off, as if his magic were a paddock fence around him. She need not have held off. His magic was gone now. It had started to wane as he slaughtered the unhatched Hatchlings, as he pounded the soul-mouse to death. 'Phelim . . . ' she began.

The ushtey would be reaching the dewponds now, or the river, or be heading on for the sea itself, its rider stuck as fast as a flea to a dog. In it would plunge and on down into the deepest, most sunless place, its hooves raising bubbles, as they had raised dust and flints, breathing water. Ever-Good Green had committed his first act of wickedness and his magic was guttering out like a spent candle.

Aisling waved away the glashans who had begun to creep forward out of the fields to peep over the wall. She put up a finger to warn away the domovoy who stood grinning, his black shoulder against the door post. 'How are you, Green Boy?' she asked peaceably.

'Not so good, to be honest,' he said. 'Not so very good.' Then he breathed in deeply. 'But all right, I suppose. Just about all right.'

Also by Geraldine McCaughrean

Plundering Paradise
ISBN 0 19 271547 X

Winner of the Smarties Book Prize Bronze Award

Nathan felt his stomach cramp and his heart fill up. Go among the pirates? See pirates, in their natural habitat? They were the stuff of all his daydreams; they were the very people he had thought about all his dull childhood—the beacons that had lit his way through every bleak, grey day of his bleak, grey life. But did he want to meet any? Did he really want to see the genuine item?

Nathan's daydreams about pirates come to an abrupt end when he is summoned to see the headmaster of his school, only to be told that two terms' fees have not been paid and he must leave the school immediately.

When Tamo White—the son of a pirate—suggests that Nathan go home with him to Madagascar, it seems to Nathan as if his daydreams might come true—but then he remembers his sister, Maud. How could he take 'Mousy Maud' to a strange land, peopled by savages and home to cut-throats and pirates? But Maud seems to like the idea . . .

'The story develops its own rollicking momentum . . . her Madagascar springs off the page, equatorial, relaxed, full of exotic flowers, animals and superstitions.'
Daily Telegraph

Forever X
ISBN 0 19 271748 0

Shortlisted for the Carnegie Medal

The old man lunged through, scattering the Shepherds off the doormat, and made for the barn, head down saying, 'Merry Christmas! Merry Christmas, one and all, yes.'

When the Shepherds' car breaks down on the way to their summer holiday, the only place they can find to stay is Forever Xmas, the hotel where every day is Christmas day.

Mr and Mrs Shepherd would like to give the festivities a miss; four-year-old Mel wants to enter into them heart and soul. Joy is not sure how she should react, but when she makes friends with Holly, the resident elf, she can't help being drawn in to the strange Partridge household.

Then Mr Angel arrives, and the police, and Christmas will never be the same again!

'a sharply plotted farce with only one joke, but lots of punchlines and acid undertones.'
The Times Educational Supplement

'a stunningly clever novel'
Books For Keeps

Gold Dust

ISBN 0 19 271721 9

Winner of the 1994 Beefeater Children's Novel Award.

Inez and her brother Maro were amazed to see a big hole being dug outside their father's shop. Their amazement grew when so many other holes appeared in the main street that the traffic couldn't use it any more.

Then the rumours began to spread. Someone said they had glimpsed the mythical alicanto bird which eats gold and glows with the brightness of it. Someone else had seen the carbunco with its double shell which opens to take in fresh supplies of its favourite food—gold.

It was starting up all over again—the frantic rush for gold, the time of rumour and raised hopes, of exaggeration and lies, of racing against time to find a piece of ground where no one's pick had fallen yet.

This exciting novel, set in modern-day Brazil, paints a wild and exuberant picture of two children, their family, and a host of eccentric characters all caught up in gold fever.

'a rip-roaring adventure, full of vigorous, stylish writing and hilarious happenings.'

The Times Educational Supplement

Re-issued in the Oxford Children's Modern Classics series

A Pack of Lies
ISBN 0 19 271788 X

When MCC Berkshire moves into Ailsa and her mother's antique shop, he turns their lives upside down. He sleeps on the old bed that's for sale in the shop, and corners every potential customer with a special story, told just for them. But where does MCC come from? And why does he tell such awful lies?

Ailsa has never met anyone like this. Adventure, horror, romance, comedy, tragedy, mystery—MCC tells a pack of lies to suit every taste. But then he is, after all, the real joker in the pack.

This witty and fascinating collection was awarded both the Guardian Children's Fiction Award and the Carnegie Medal.

'The sheer glee of the enterprise is irresistible.'

The Times Educational Supplement

A Little Lower than the Angels
ISBN 0 19 271780 4

Gabriel is worth twenty shillings as an apprentice to the stonemason. It is an uncertain, dangerous life—until God Himself, in the shape of playmaster Garvey, reaches out a helping hand. But will the new life be any more secure, overshadowed by such figures as the Devil and his scowling daughter?

In a world of illusion, people are not always what they seem. Least of all Gabriel.

A Little Lower than the Angels won the 1987 Whitbread Children's Novel Award.

'A fine children's book because of the emotional power of the storytelling, unflinching and true.'

Books for Your Children